Alice Ash is a writer and ███████ was longlisted for the G████████ writing has been featured in *Granta*, *Hotel*, *3:AM Magazine*, the *TLS* and *Extra Teeth*, among others. *Paradise Block* was shortlisted for the 2021 Edge Hill Short Story Prize. She lives in Brighton.

Praise for *Paradise Block*:

'A powerful testimony to the reality of life on the margins. Raw, bizarre, disturbing, funny and uncanny'
Cathy Sweeney, author of *Modern Times*

'Engaging, funny and surprising in equal measure, these stories are the work of a wonderfully unconventional imagination'
Laura Kaye, author of *English Animals*

'This is not a green and pleasant land, but something much more prevalent, overlooked and deeply English. These stories depict difficult, often cash-poor characters, but they are respectfully written with such texture and poetry that they give voice to the thousands of lives that they echo. Eclectic, dark, moving and sometimes very funny'
Kate Sawyer, author of *The Stranding*

'Lively, unerring, intimate and gorgeously grotesque! Sentences as satisfying as feeling the cool squish of silt between your toes. As you merrily connect the dots between crisscrossing lives, these stories will get under your skin and make themselves at home there'
Gemma Reeves, author of *Victoria Park*

Paradise Block

ALICE ASH

This paperback edition first published in 2022

First published in Great Britain in 2021 by Serpent's Tail,
an imprint of PROFILE BOOKS LTD
29 Cloth Fair
London
EC1A 7JQ
www.serpentstail.co.uk

10 9 8 7 6 5 4 3 2 1

Typset in Freight Text by MacGuru Ltd
Designed by Barneby Ltd
Printed and bound in Great Britain by
CPI Group (UK) Ltd, Croydon, CR0 4YY

The moral right of the author has been asserted.

A CIP record for this book can be obtained from the British Library

ISBN 978 1 78816 555 6
eISBN 978 1 78283 722 0

For Nanny and her magical train.

Contents

Eggs

It is very early on, still the beginning. I am still the daughter. *She* is still the mother. I can run through the flat while *She* sobs over pink laundry. *One red sock.* I don't care; I am running to my bedroom with headphones in my ears, hiding for one, two, three hours, listening to the music. There are four different cassettes: all albums by my favourite artist. It is Robbie Williams. Some smells and screaming come under the door, but I have been forgotten about and I can hide with the cassettes, listen with the headphones: *Robbie Williams*.

When the cassette ends I turn it over quickly, press play, but during the brief silence I hear screaming, and I accidentally glance at Little Vincent. His skin is red and mottled; he has a rash and his face opens up, like a wound: I can see his wet tongue thrashing around inside. He screams and I turn, swivel my eyes around the room; the doorway, where the grey smoke is pouring in.

I can talk to other girls about Robbie Williams; I can think about him when I get home from school. There is one song I like, one song in particular; it is about a girl with the same name as me, but she is a completely different girl.

Little Vincent says, 'Can't breathe.'

And I don't hear him, but I accidentally read his lips, see him coughing. I try to concentrate on the music, the peace-making angels giving themselves away, Robbie Williams; but Little Vincent has swung his fat legs over the side of his bunk and is kicking his boots against the wood. He wants me to do something. There is a fire in her room, and *She* is screaming especially loud. I can hear her, even when the fire alarm starts, even though Robbie Williams is shouting, 'I'M LOVING ANGELS INSTEAD.'

Without thinking about what it will mean, I pick up Little Vincent, and run down the stairs.

Min is worried that her flat next door will be burnt, but the firefighters come quickly and use their twisting hoses on the spluttering flames that want to reach up and touch the big yellow letters that say PARADISE BLOCK. They look awkwardly at where my mother's dress has been burnt. *She* is leaning against the building, her ears covered against the fire alarm, the tattered white material billowing around her naked legs and feet.

Min tries to clean my brother's face with a bit of tissue.

'What's this red?' she says. 'Is that a rash?'

Min never listens to anyone; she asks these questions, but she doesn't want to hear the answers. Whatever Min is doing, she is always in motion, always about to move on to her next task. Min is rubbing at my brother's rash, her eyes are very worried; but moments later she is dusting down the wall where some dirt has touched the cream paint.

'Well,' she says, and she reaches down to snatch at some weeds whose heads have grown up between the bricks, to shoo some of the white cats that are gathering quickly.

I put my headphones back on.

She is crying, covered with a silver blanket. Three women stand around her nervously. One of the women reaches out and timidly strokes her hair. Min has finished with the weeds and the cats, and she leans over me to take off my headphones.

'You should help your mother,' she says.

I can see that her hands want to fuss me, to adjust my dress, push me towards my mother, but for a moment she is still. We are watching Little Vincent, who is pissing up against the front of Paradise Block, just underneath our downstairs window, where the fire has been raging. The fire alarm stops very suddenly, but he continues. Little Vincent is pissing into the smoke, coughing and laughing, as if this is a game. The smoke pours out from our downstairs window like a black tongue.

The headphones have lost their power. I can listen to Robbie Williams, the outside sounds are not part of it, but now darkness invades the *inside* of the music.

There is a cup of water in my room; it is old and grey. The water vibrates, and I know that something is happening downstairs, within the guts of the flat. I take off one headphone, just to see, and I can hear her. *She* is changing, scratching on my door. Little Vincent is crying.

'I won't open it,' I say, but I know that outside there is the black hallway and my mother, crawling on the floor.

The flat is very burnt, and women keep coming and bringing little gifts. These gifts stand out brightly against the charcoal, and this makes the women feel bad, as though the gifts were designed to make the flat look worse, as though that's their fault. *She* cries every time they bring something new. They don't know whether *She* is crying happy tears or sad ones, because *She* always looks the same: head back, mouth open. *She* howls.

Min has brought me a present of my own. It is a shiny pink apron. On the apron there are words, curling white and maggoty letters: 'Little Lady'. Min holds the apron in front of my face until I am forced to look at it. She slips the string over my head and ties the back securely with a double knot.

I take Little Vincent to school the next day. He skips and sings a song happily: 'Jack and Jill went up the hill, To fetch a pail of water, Jack fell down and broke his crown, And Jill came tumbling after.' His voice is very sweet and his hand is tiny. We are on time for school and the teacher gives my brother a gold star to wear on his jumper.

My brother says, 'I won!'

Everything is okay, but I wake up at midnight because my brother is screaming. I get into bed with him and he clings to me. I cannot sleep and during the night *She* slips into the room and sees us.

She gets into the bed next to me. 'Hush, hush, my babies. Mother is here.'

And then *She* starts crying, but *She* does it with Little Vincent's toy bird stuffed in her mouth, so I can just hear the heaving. *She* falls asleep on top of my arm and shoulder, and I watch the plastic stars that my brother has stuck to the blackened ceiling. The stars are supposed to be glow-in-the-dark, but they aren't glowing at all. Maybe the curtains are not thick enough to make the room properly dark.

Now, Min comes around and shows me how to make eggs. She delivers the instructions as though to herself.

'It doesn't do for the water to be simmering,' Min says. 'Make the water lively; make it really boil.'

I think that Min might have forgotten that I am in the room, and that this is how she always makes eggs, muttering to herself, staring into the bubbling water, measuring the spot to hit the knife against the orange shell.

I watch Min carefully, and I learn how to take the eggs out of the water, where they are smashing their bodies against the edge of the pan. Min waits for the moment when the eggs are no longer hot, places them carefully in their pale blue eggcups. She cuts the eggs' heads off, pushing the knife towards her thumb until the blunt metal hits her thumb skin. She stares at the eggs for a few seconds and then walks away and out of our flat.

Min never eats the eggs herself.

I make eggs every day that week, and Little Vincent is less irritable. His rash disappears, and now his face is round and softly white. Even *She* takes one of the eggs and dips a piece of hard bread into its eye.

'I love eggs,' *She* says.

'Me too,' my brother agrees.

There is less screaming now, just damp sounds as Little Vincent sucks and chews. *She* is happy, trying to paint the burnt walls with tubes of watercolour paint. *She* has wrapped her head in a silk scarf, and *She* keeps retying it to trap her giant yellow hair inside. Beneath her big head, *She* looks smaller and *She* moves around more, sometimes almost leaping. *She* chatters about writing letters and replying to important people, but when *She* is working, I see that *She* is just practising her signature, turning the loops and smiling. It is peaceful; there is less screaming, and I can hum Robbie Williams to myself while I make the eggs.

But that evening, I find something strange. It is just a cluster of lines behind my knee. At first, I think that Little Vincent has used a felt tip to draw on me while I was sleeping, but the lines are very fine and faint, and they won't disappear when I rub them with spit. They are light green, like the threads in my wrist, and when it has been a few days, I realise that this is something from inside, something coming to the surface. I tell the lines to go away, go back inside, but soon they get darker, and then they come undone; they begin to spool around to the front of my calf. Now the threads appear like a ball of wool, a huge cloud underneath my knee. The cloud is a dark purple scribble with floating green threads, swirling up and into my thigh. The threads are not painful, but they are ugly and strange. Before I help Little Vincent into his pyjamas, I steal a pair of the long beige stockings that are always drying on Min's washing line.

At school, we are making cards for Mother's Day. I shade mine carefully, working on covering one tiny corner with flowers. I am hunched over, keeping my eyes close to the paper. I want every inch of the card to be covered; there will be no empty white space. I am concentrating very hard when I realise that the teacher is standing by my desk.

'Lovely,' he says, but he seems nervous and tries to talk to me about the fire and how much of our stuff was burnt, whether the rest of the block set alight.

I tell him, 'Little Vincent is still alive, if that's what you want to know,' and he laughs, as if I have told a joke.

'Well,' the teacher says, sliding his watch up and down his thin wrist, 'if you ever want to talk about it.'

When the bell rings for break my card is only one-quarter finished, and I cover the rest of the paper quickly, with light green threads and a threatening angry cloud in a purple colour that nearly matches my leg spool.

Min is there, looking over on to our balcony.

She nods twice and pats the concrete approvingly when she sees that I am putting out the washing.

'You *should* be helping your mother,' she says.

'I am,' I reply.

My brother's small underpants and my mother's billowy white dresses. The dresses shriek around like ghosts on the washing line and inside I can hear screaming again.

When I am finished, I slump down amongst the plant pots. There is a crack in the wall, so I watch Min scolding her little dog, Missy. I wonder whether Missy knows that she is being scolded because she rolls on to her back and shows her yellow tummy. Min is drying many pairs of stockings on her washing line, as well as some of her husband's long black trousers, and she walks up and down, weaving in and out of the hanging legs.

I am nearly going back inside, but then I notice something strange on Min's leg. Min is wearing a pair of the stockings, so I can't be sure, but I think that I can see it, the spool, the purple storm on Min's skin, brewing and blistering, much larger than mine. Min turns around to crush a spider that is hanging from one of her pots, and I see that there is a scribble on her other leg too, creeping out from underneath the hem of her skirt.

She is looking through her papers for something when I get back from school, her little hands scattering the sheets.

'Where is it, where is it?' *She* yelps.

She is crying.

'What are you looking for?' I say, and I touch her.

She leaps backwards.

'Who the hell are you?' *She* says, and we stare at each other.

She has threaded bits of ribbon through the light-coloured plaits that are on either side of her head, and *She* wears a glass necklace that I had been hiding inside my pillowcase.

'What?' I say.

I drop my school bag on the floor and it makes a thudding sound.

'Oh.' *She* is brushing the golden hair from her forehead, dabbing her bright eyes with her sleeve.

'It's so dark in here,' *She* whimpers. 'Why is it so dark?'

She begins to cry again.

My brother is doing very well at school and he comes home with a second gold star. He sits at the table, greedily eating eggs. *She* is working feverishly over her papers and says *She* hasn't got time when I ask her if *She* wants an egg for herself. I don't know what *She* is doing, and I try to look by walking past her several times, back and forth. The fire has burnt many of the papers, and *She* is taping pieces together carefully, like a surgeon, her tongue sticking out.

Later, a siren starts up somewhere down the road, and I think that the screaming has begun again, or that there is another fire, but when I look, *She* is still working on the papers, scribbling notes with her sparkly pen and putting numbers into her calculator.

She smiles with her small mouth when *She* sees me, and says, 'Mother will take care of everything.'

She is so pleased that *She* keeps laughing quietly, giggling and then shushing herself, as though *She* is very clever to have a secret plan.

I go to my room and wait.

I am wearing my headphones, but now I can barely hear my music above the screaming. *She* is there, in the middle of the burnt kitchen. *She* is wearing my favourite party dress, which barely fits me any more but isn't even tight on her small body, and I can see that *She* has been trying to make a Special Meal: eggs sliced into strange shapes and placed across slices of black bread.

There is blood all over her hands.

'She shouldn't be doing it,' Min says.

She has taken my headphones away, but she is not talking directly to me: she talks to a woman. They are all standing inside our burnt flat.

'It is too much for her,' Min says.

Min has given my mother a pill to eat and *She* holds it in her damaged hand for a moment before *She* swallows it.

'Everything will be okay, dear,' Min says kindly; she pats her arm like it is an animal. *She* nods her head limply and lets out a giant sigh, hugging herself while the women crowd around her. *She* looks tiny, like a child. I try to follow the shadows around the edge of the flat, to get to where the stairs are, but I am too big now – Min sees me and she grabs hold of my shoulders. Her eyes are swirling and blue. Min goes to get my apron. It is hanging on a hook, a shining pink pig.

'Don't be selfish,' she yelps, forcing the plastic material into my hands, waiting until I put the apron on.

'You're the little lady now,' Min tells me, and she gives me a little push, towards the blackened kitchen. 'You're the mother,' she says.

The blood has been washed and the knife put away, but there are still a few pinkish pieces of egg left on the chopping board. The papers remain, strewn across the table, and I look at the printed letters, which talk about money and demands, but are disordered and change into nonsense along the seams, where they have been taped. I see my mother's purple notes. Her writings look like flowers or small animals but not like the actual words that are needed.

On the hob there are three pans, chattering and bouncing as they boil over and spill their contents. I stare at my hands very hard, willing myself away, but without my headphones I can hear the pans banging, like intruders running up and down the stairs. I can hear the screaming of my brother, the heaving. I can see my brother's scars, his rash has returned; his hair is hopping with head lice. *She* holds her damaged hand to her chest, whimpering and sighing. One of the pans begins to screech and I go to the hob and turn the fire off. Against the blackness of the burnt rooms my family is very vibrant and I cannot look away.

Little Vincent has grown three inches, and he can reach the showerhead to wash himself now, although he does not.

'What would your friends say if they knew your sister helps you in the bath?' I ask him, but he just stares at me and brings his flat hand down in the water, making a splash that goes all over me. Suddenly, we can hear my breath coming up from my chest, it is rattling when it comes out of my mouth. I wheeze like an old person and fold over the side of the bath. My brother looks at me, out of his little face.

'Stop doing that now,' he demands, but I can't, and I grab at my throat.

'Stop it,' he says again.

It is nearly Christmas, and now my brother comes home with a different kind of star, one that he has made for the top of the tree. I go on to the balcony to find a tall branch. There are only small twigs and they are wet and useless, but there is a sapling cowering in a corner, surrounded by weeds and bits of broken china.

Little Vincent stands in the doorway, holding his star with both hands, while I dig in a circle, almost to the edges of the pot. This is as far as I can imagine the little tree's veins stretching, and then I dig further down. I picture the tree being released in a great brown ball of tangled seething. But then, there is a thick vein, and it seems like it keeps moving around, thrashing from side to side to avoid my spade, or maybe there are many thick roots. I have to be very quick and dig very fast, and while I am doing so, I feel something popping inside of my spine, and a white spool of pain unties inside, and I am lying on the wet ground.

I am doing very badly at school and the teacher has sent a Note of Concern home, but the next few weeks are spent in bed with tablets that make the mind quiet, whispering to me only occasionally about eggs and stars. In the Plum Regis hospital, I have a stick to help me move around.

The doctor is surprised when she removes my stolen stockings and sees my legs; and she touches them all over with her little plastic gloves. She gives me an injection and then I hear her talking about my spools to another man doctor in the corridor. This doctor has an accent and a voice like a tape slowing when the batteries have run down: 'Un-u-sual in some-onnne so yooou-ng,' he says. 'Vari-coo-se veeei-ns and miiiild arth-i-ri-tis?' he asks, as though this is a question, and then I find that I have been asleep because my eyes are opening and the corridor is empty.

It is Christmassy in the hospital, and a man wearing a red jacket and trousers and a fake white beard comes into my room. He asks me to confirm my name and wants to know how old I am before he starts dancing around at the end of my bed. I am baffled by all of this and I ask the man what he wants from me. After he has given me a tiny sewing kit: needles and three different colours of thread; even a tiny thimble that is too small for my first finger, he leaves the room looking angry.

My brother has stolen the teacher's sticker book and he has gold stars all over the front of his jumper and some on his face and hands. He has time off school now, and he sits and watches me. Someone has brought me grapes, and he eats them all and leaves the tiny pips across the edge of my blanket. It is like a trail of snot.

Min comes.

'Your mother is very upset,' she tells me, picking grape pips from the blanket. She holds the pips in her hand.

'What were you doing, trying to dig that tree up?' Min asks.

When I am home again, some women bring a Christmas pudding. I try to see if these women have marks on their legs, but they are wearing trousers or long skirts and stockings. *She* says that *She* will set fire to the pudding, and the women all look sideways at each other. I am still walking with the stick; I feel too nervous to support my weight, and I like the sound that the stick makes as I tap around the flat. It is like someone is walking around with me, helping me with my household tasks.

Little Vincent has balled up many sheets of paper and arranged them all to make a kind of tree formation. He has put the star on top and is pouring a tin of green paint over the paper. The screaming starts when *She* sees what he is doing and realises that the papers he has used are her special papers, the ones that *She* has been poring over. While they scream, I find a bottle of my mother's dental fluid and empty it over the pudding. There is a huge flame, nearly to the black ceiling. The pudding burns for a long time and when it goes out, the cake that is left is chewy, tasting minty and rich.

Two men come and they keep buzzing through the morning while *She* tries to sleep. It is hard for me to get into her room since this is where the fire started and the door has crumbled into many jagged pieces, barring my entry. *She* is smaller now and *She* can slide in and out whenever *She* wants to.

She is curled up, nearly covered by the green papers; streaks of green paint are on her arms and legs. I can see that *She* is wearing her eye mask, the one with hearts and shells patterned on the silk, and that *She* has her hands over her ears. There are candles all over the floor, white and milky, like bones. *She* is beautiful and very still, like a painting, not a real mother or woman, and soft orange light is coming in through her window, resting on her body like a blanket.

The buzzing continues, and I can hear Min at the front of the building, in the car park; she is asking the people what they want, but when they try to tell her, she just starts screaming. I hear scuffling and feel my brother's clammy hand on my arm. He is peering through, into the room, where *She* lies. Little Vincent starts to scream and, quite suddenly, my mother stands up, straight as a pin, and I can see a thin black line around her neck, reaching up under her hair.

I realise that *She* is wearing headphones.

There are two men there; one is wearing a plastic card attached to his trousers by a long stretchy string, which he pulls out to show us before it pings back to his waistband. My brother stops screaming and laughs, he tries to reach for the plastic card again, but the man steps backwards into the puddle of swamp water that has gathered in the middle of the step. The man looks annoyed and the second man is behind him, peering at our flat, which is stained black, a blemish on the face of Paradise Block.

'We are looking for the home owner,' this second man says, 'which one of you is the home owner?'

He reads the address, 'Flat 4, Paradise Block, Box Close, Clutter', even though he is standing on the doorstep, right in front of us.

She is picking at a streak of green paint on her knee, and her white gown is billowing around her small body.

The man in the puddle starts talking: 'We have been trying to reach you,' he says. 'You have not been replying to our letters. If you do not meet our demands, we will be forced to seize your property.'

I look at my mother to see if *She* will respond, but *She* is still looking at the paint, tracing the line from her sock to the place under her nightgown, fascinated, and when I look back at the man, I see that he is actually looking at me, not my mother, and that now he is very angry.

'Do you have anything to say for yourself?' he asks me, and I have no way of replying, so I just lean on my stick and say, 'I am very sorry, sir.'

She has my headphones on when I get home from school. I want to know what *She* is listening to, but *She* can't hear me, and my voice starts to tremble and crack when I shout. I go to the kitchen and make eggs for Little Vincent and for her, and when I have finished clearing away, they shout, 'MORE EGGS,' and I look and see that they have finished them already.

I try to talk to the other girls about Robbie Williams, although, without my headphones, I can hardly remember his voice or what he liked to sing about. A girl is wearing a Robbie Williams T-shirt under her school blouse; I can see his eyes through the thin material.

'Why do you have a stick like an old person?' the girl asks me.

One morning, I wake up and feel very tired still, although I have slept for a long time. I can't hear any screaming, and I look at the top bunk to see if my brother is still asleep. Perhaps we all have a great tiredness.

Little Vincent is not in his bed, but I can hear some noises outside and when I look out of the window, I can see my mother and my brother from far away, almost at the bus stop. I have not seen her taking Little Vincent to school for a long time and so I am surprised. As I watch, I see them step into the road in front of a giant lorry. They jump backwards, back on to the pavement. I think that they are laughing. Before they cross the road, I see that *She* is wearing my school uniform.

When they get home from school, I shout to my mother, 'What the hell do you think you are doing?' but *She* just looks at me vaguely and points to a gold star on the front of her cardigan.

'Aren't you pleased?' *She* asks me.

The two of them skulk through the flat, leaving crayons and book bags against the black walls and floor. My mother is singing Robbie Williams and dancing a little bit.

I begin to scream, but *She* does not hear me and Little Vincent looks at me for a few seconds with a distant interest, before he points his small finger to the centre of my pink apron and says, 'Eggs,' and then he begins to scream also.

Planes

Benny has freckles across his nose, like a handful of sand, and there are still dimples in his cheeks, although his face is getting older, longer, and he has a number-three haircut, shaved quite close on the sides. Standing in the hallway between his bedroom and his mother's room, he has a model plane that he holds, squeezing the body. Benny imagines that the plane windows might come tinkling out. There is sudden violent barking, coming from outside, and Benny releases the plane; it falls on to the floor, lands in a pile of his mother's clothes: blouses and jumpers that look like a volcanic landscape. The passengers are screaming as the plane dissolves into a pair of large, plum-coloured knickers. Benny looks at the marks that the plane has left on his palm; the red ridges, and then he hears his mother coming up the stairs, her voice singing into her telephone, her false laughter; her red slippies scuffling, grumbling through the carpet.

Benny Dodd
25 Wish Drive
Plum Regis

Hi Dad,

I know it's been a long time and you are so busy, but actually, I've got to talk to you. I'm stuck here with Elaine the Liar, and pretty soon I'm going to lose it, go completely mad, or something.

Elaine goes out to the department store and even to collect me from school wearing bad old clothes and every day these horrible plastic slippies. She gets these slippies from the job that she has on the phones, where she works for a company called Deelite, lying and lying (which is what she does best), making sadsacks believe that they have won really good prizes because of a scratch card, when actually, in real life, the prizes are total rubbish. The sadsacks are so busy listening to Elaine about what prizes they're getting in the post that they forget to hang up the phone, even though the call costs £3.75 per minute, and I'm telling you, Dad, these prizes are not even worth one amount of £3.75.

EXAMPLE: a set of playing cards with naked ladies on the front. The cards are really disgusting, one of the Worst Things. Elaine keeps all her Deelite rubbish in a cupboard under the stairs, and I cover my eyes if one of the cards has been left out or something. I just stand there and shout for Elaine until she comes and takes it away.

And this is how I know Elaine is a compulsive liar, which is someone who can't even help lying, because that's how good she is, that she can make someone, some sadsack, believe that those naked-ladies cards are a good thing to get delivered to your house through the post. Another 'prize' is a cheese-coloured cowboy hat with a red ribbon and 'giddy-up' printed on the side, and honestly, anyone who tried to wear *that* would look like a freakin' idiot, even a real cowboy. The last thing to tell you about is a set of three plastic babies, each one smaller than the other one, and the last one is as small as a slug. I always find the slug-baby in weird places, even though the babies are each wrapped in plastic, the little one always gets out, escapes. There was one slug-baby behind the toilet. I saw another one under the sofa when I was looking for the TV remote.

Then there are the red slippies that she wears to school or to the department store until they are broken, and then she takes a new pair from where she keeps the 'prizes', in the cupboard under the stairs, and just throws the old ones into the bin outside. Dad, Elaine doesn't even recycle like the other mums or care about the plastic in the sea, which will cause very bad harm to Planet Earth.

There's a boy called Jake Standing in my class who has dogs that are trained to run and to bite people, but not me because we're sort of best friends, and he smashed a window when Miss Mitchelmore wouldn't let him go out at break-time. Once he'd done that window-smashing we had to watch a film about a boy who jumped in front of a train, and Miss Mitchelmore had to put a special cardboard box in the corner of the classroom. This is called 'The Feelings Space' and you can write something and not even say your name. I wrote about a very frightening train that I imagined, running towards all the other children with big white wheels and teeth, and the next day Miss Mitchelmore kept on asking me about my feelings when I was trying to get on with my work, writing facts about the dangers of plane crashes. She basically asked me to stay behind at break and gave me a small packet of liquorice sweets for free and a bottle of milk, and said she was worried, and if you're wondering how she knew it was me who wrote about the train, Dad, she said that she saw my handwriting, and also that she could tell from the way I had been acting in class the whole time. Miss Mitchelmore asked me if I had some 'strange or disturbing thoughts', and I said, yes, obviously (because, think about it, Dad, what with the naked-ladies cards and the slug-babies, and the mum who is constantly lying).

So now Miss Mitchelmore is basically the only one who cares about me, apart from you, obviously, Dad. And even with Elaine's compulsive lying she hasn't been able to tell a big enough lie to make me think that you are a bad dad, the Bad Dad she always talks about. I know all about the planes that you fly and how you can't just come and see me all the time, like you want to, because piloting is such an important job. I can imagine flying in the sky and how that will feel and how far away you will go and be. Sometimes I go to this little park on top of a hill, a really good place for seeing planes, and I spend hours watching the sky, thinking that I might see a Sunny Air plane going over and away from Plum Regis.

But anyway, I don't think it's right to lie to your son or flesh+blood, and I just wanted you to know what Elaine has been doing and how much worse she is now even than when you knew her, most probably. And thanks for the birthday presents, the planes that you send me, I already wrote to say thanks. Did you get that letter, Dad? Elaine won't tell me the address or how to contact you, but I worked it out by myself. I just looked up 'Sunny Air' on the internet because of how there is 'Sunny Air' written on the planes that you send. I have taken the planes into school to show my class, especially Jake Standing. Jake's brothers breed dogs for running at the dog track and they sometimes come and bark by the gate. I told Jake about how you are a pilot and showed him what kind of planes you fly. So I do like the planes, but considering it's going to be my tenth birthday, Dad, maybe you could come and see me, or even come and get me, and then I can live with you? I can understand why you couldn't live with Elaine any more, Dad – I feel exactly the same!

I've put some facts about what you look like on a separate sheet, just in case the person who opens this letter (hi person, if you're reading) might not know your name, in a big company like Sunny Air. But maybe they do know what you look like, and they can find you. I have a painting of you and I nearly put it in with this letter, but then, I am worried that I will forget what you look like. Elaine will lie and tell me you look like something else, something completely different. I keep my painting next to the planes and Elaine basically laughs at me when she sees it. Not laughs, but smiles, smirks, you know. I can't believe that you used to be married to Elaine, Dad! She is always laughing at your picture and calling you Bad Dad. Julie comes over and they smoke and drink pink wine, which is bad for your body, and I have to sit and listen to them going on about how you hardly send any money and other lies that I won't even say here (but they are about s*x).

And I haven't even told you the worst bit yet, because I am embarrassed in actual fact, but oh well this is it: Elaine talks to men on the phone as well. The other thing she works for is called 'S*x for You' and she talks to all these men, so disgusting. One time I picked up the phone in her bedroom and listened to her talking for only a few minutes, and I was nearly sick, and then Elaine heard me breathing on the line and she was screaming at me downstairs, but that's how I know for sure that she is a compulsive liar, because she says her name is *Sandy*, and talks for ages about what she is wearing. I don't know how to tell you this, Dad, but Elaine says that she is s*xy and that she is wearing this s*xy underwear, and that she is only 25 years old, and all this time she is roughly 40–45 years old, and she is wearing the red plastic slippies and this grey fluffy dressing gown that she has on every single day. She hardly even wears clothes these days, Dad, only when she has to come and get me from school, and even then she wears the slippies, and doesn't brush her hair or put on any lipstick. It's not a good place for a young boy and let's be serious, what if I turn out like her: a compulsive s*x-liar.

As you know, it is my birthday on Friday, so send me a plane if you want to. I do really like the planes. But also, please come and get me if you can and you're not too far away right now, but if you are far away, just come a bit later.

So now I'll see you soon or in a little time longer than soon.

Thanks, Dad, that's great.

Your son,

Benny John Dodd

PS I forgot to tell you that Jake Standing has scars all over his face from wrestling a dog and he even has a bone that he can pop out of his leg and then back in again from an accident in his brother's lorry, when five other cars were crashed and they were all on fire!

Elaine is on the phone and Benny is melting the nose of one of his model planes on the hob. Elaine has to work on the phone, and Benny is left to himself for a few hours, even though it is his birthday today. Benny watches the nose of his plane wilting from the heat and the chewing-gum substance that falls from the body.

Benny receives a plane for his birthday every year from his father, and now he can't decide whether he wants to treasure the planes, keeping them all along his bedroom windowsill, or burn them, smashing off their wings with the little hammer that his mother keeps by the front door.

He can hear Elaine: 'Oh yeah, you know how I like it.' She is stripping wallpaper in her bedroom and talking on the phone. She sounds like an American woman. Benny doesn't like how his mother can shift like this, change into a different person from one minute to the next. Benny stares hard at a lorry that is stopped outside, a group of men. The men are all packed into the front seat and they don't look at Benny, where he stands by the kitchen window. He watches them, though, and he sees that Jake Standing is sat amongst them, a little stick figure, a bony lump of greyhound on his lap.

Jake climbs down from the cab making angry gestures, walking up the road with the dog, towards the park on the hill. This park has a very good vantage point for watching planes, and Benny often goes to gaze up at their compact bellies, thinking he might see a Sunny Air plane; that he might wave to his father. Benny cranes his neck, hoping that Jake won't walk up the dusty path to the park, that he won't discover his special place. Jake is holding several brown packages and the lorry blows past him, shouting, 'Don't come home until you've posted 'em,' and—

Benny jumps as the flame consumes the plane suddenly and he drops the white lump of plastic into the sink.

Benny Dodd
25 Wish Drive
Plum Regis

Hi Dad,

Thanks for the plane, but guess what happened? There was a fight at school and I was just sat there reading a book about engines and science, but then Jake Standing – that's the boy with the greyhound dogs and the knee that got smashed up in a fight or a car crash – he must've thought that my bag belonged to someone else, because he took it and emptied it on to the floor. I was there screaming at him, but some of the cards I was telling you about, the disgusting naked-ladies ones, they fell out of the bag! I honestly don't know how they got there, I even thought that Elaine might have put them in my bag, to make me feel embarrassed, but anyway, her plan worked, because I was *so* embarrassed. I had to go into the toilets at lunchtime and stay there, even though it was my birthday and on birthday days Miss Mitchelmore brings in cupcakes, which is pretty much the only nice or good thing about my school.

So now all the boys, and even some of the girls, they have the cards and they get them out and wave them around, and I just feel sick sick sick. And I know that I shouldn't have, but I told those idiots that I didn't care anyway, because you were going to fly a Sunny Air plane to come and get me, probably before the end of next week. So now I suppose the pressure really is on for you to come right away.

Sorry about that, Dad, but that means I really will see you soon, probably.

Your son,
Benny John Dodd

PS I forgot to say that Elaine only gave me a bag of marbles from Deelite for my birthday. I also forgot to tell you properly that she is *obsessed* with money and she is always going on about how you never send anything, but I know that all she is doing is just trying to turn me against you, pretending that you are the Bad Dad.

And also, Dad, I know about this secret stash of money that she has at the back of the cutlery drawer, just keeping it for herself – there's hundreds of pounds in there! I said to her once that she doesn't spend any money on me anyway cos she's so stingy, getting all my birthday presents out of the cupboard under the stairs, and she slapped my face and pretended to have a bath even though I checked the hot water, and it wasn't even on, so she couldn't have been having a bath! She can't even tell the truth about that ...

I am waiting for your reply and it's my birthday, so that's my birthday wish – reply!

Benny is ten years old: old enough to babysit for the family next door, who often look over the wall to see how Benny is getting on, smiling and complimenting him on his planes and the star jumps that he likes to practise out there, reaching fifty, sometimes nearly a hundred. This babysitting job is really just sitting in front of the TV while Elaine works on the phone. When Benny's mother is on the sofa in front of their own TV next door, which she mostly is, Benny can sometimes hear her voice, talking to the Sex for You men. The houses in this part of Plum Regis are built very sparely and the family next door have their sofa in nearly the same spot as Benny and his mum, on the other side of the wall.

Sometimes Benny starts to get lulled by Elaine's voice, because it's past 10 p.m., and he has been up to check on the little girl three times (seen her chest moving up and down, the cocoa that Benny had prepared for her himself still staining the corners of her very small mouth), and he has decided to stop being worried about her. Benny eats the snack that has been left out for him: black bread and honey, two shiny discs of liquorice, stamped like a coin. He eats some red jam out of a jar that he finds, and then smooths the glistening surface with his finger, so that you can't tell.

Benny is lulled and not worried about the girl; he is peacefully full of food, and because it is 10.30 p.m., a game show is on. It is an American game show and a blonde woman wears a blindfold; she has to find a clue with her mouth in a bowl full of water, and what she doesn't know is that the clues in the bowl are all shaped like long penises, and the audience is laughing at her. Benny is so lulled, listening to his mother's voice, the comforting grumble, and the bad words popping out of the darkness: COCK, FUCK, HARD, watching the woman trying to catch one of the penises with her tongue, the red jam sweetness and the honey inside of his own mouth. Benny flips over on to his belly and his part finds a groove between the sofa cushions. He pretends to himself that he is going to sleep, listening to his mum, dreaming of this blonde woman, but then there is a fierce kick in his stomach, and shame rolls across the walls of the family next door's house, baleful wet clouds. The woman has won 4 penis clues, and has her blindfold taken off, says, 'Oh my God.' She is giggling and the audience are all laughing, but in her eyes she is clearly upset or annoyed.

Elaine continues receiving calls, even when Benny puts a cushion over his ear, even when he finds the cartoons that are way too young for him, and sits close to the television, pretending to be enthralled by the bright colours and skipping creatures, even when he goes upstairs to perch at the edge of the little girl's bed, picking up a stuffed clown and holding it to his chest. Benny thinks about how the girl isn't even really a person yet, how everything she does is watched over and decided for her; and he wishes he could be just like her, that he could be the tiniest baby there was, tinier even than the nail on this little girl's smallest toe.

Benny Dodd
25 Wish Drive
Plum Regis

Hi Dad,
So I've been ten for a week now and things have been getting worse every single day.

I'm not a s*x pervert, at least not yet (maybe come and get me soon, though?), but Miss Mitchelmore found one of the cards – you know, the ones with the naked ladies? It was under a desk and even though it wasn't *my* desk, Jake Standing told the teacher that they were my cards, and said that I showed them to everyone and now the whole class hates me, as well as the teacher herself.

Elaine had to come into school and we sat with Miss Mitchelmore in this little room they call the Pow-Wow Room and we had milk in plastic cups and White Fingers biscuits with no chocolate on them. Miss Mitchelmore told Elaine that she was worried about me because of the naked-ladies playing cards, and then Miss Mitchelmore mentioned Elaine's job with S*x for You – you know, the one where she talks about being s*xy on the phone – and Elaine burst out crying!

Well, I did feel sorry for her then and I gave her a hug, but I should have known what she was up to, because then she just started on as usual, talking about you as the Bad Dad, and how you never send any money. Miss Mitchelmore must've seen that I was starting to get very angry because she said, 'I understand Benny is very proud of his dad and his work as a pilot,' and then Elaine stood up from her chair, still crying, and told Miss Mitchelmore that she was at 'breaking point', and then suddenly she shouted something about my father not even being a pilot in the first place! And obviously, I stuck up for you and told Miss Mitchelmore, yes he is, and what plane you flew and that I could even prove it when you reply to my letter, or when you actually just come to get me, to defend your honour or whatever.

When we left, Elaine was crying again, but I wouldn't talk to her until she admitted the truth about you. And while we were sitting there, in the car, with the rain coming down and Elaine sniffling and talking about trying her best with little or no money, that was when I remembered that she *did* have money, that I had found a massive bundle of money at the back of the cutlery drawer, behind the knives and forks and the random little bits of junk and fortune-telling fish and toast crumbs. I counted £220 and some more in coins. I wasn't ever going to borrow the money, but now no one at school will talk to me and I just have to listen to Elaine lying. She is still telling lies about you, Dad, holding on to me so I can't get away and telling me, *Your father is not who you think he is*.

So then I got the feeling, like the one I put in the feelings box, the train; do you remember? And thinking about that money and everything that I have to go through every day, well, I had to make a big decision. I might as well tell you, Dad – if you don't come and get me, I am going to take the money from the drawer and use it to get to Sunny Air, and then I'll just wait for you to get back from wherever your plane is flying.

Don't worry, Dad, cos I've already planned it very carefully on the internet, and I have to have a Pow-Wow with Miss Mitchelmore on Monday, so I'll just come then instead. It shouldn't be too hard to sneak out of school. I expect I'll just walk out and no one will even notice or care.

So yeah, look out for me, Dad! See you soon!

Your son,

Benny John Dodd

Benny is standing in front of the class. Miss Mitchelmore is sitting on an empty desk and nodding at him, smiling encouragingly. Benny has a picture that he has painted of his father wearing his uniform and he is holding it in front of him. There are a few naughty children in the class and one of them is Jake Standing. Jake has an earring and red trainers, even though the school uniform says black or brown shoes. His brothers breed a type of dog that can run fast and is very frightening.

Jake says, 'Don't you have a real picture?'

And Miss Mitchelmore turns around to shush him.

'Go on, Benny,' Miss Mitchelmore says, smiling still.

Benny sees that Jake is holding something in his hand that is furry, just on top of his knees, under his desk. Benny cannot remember where he is in his presentation, what he even knows about his father, and he has a bad feeling rising; he puts his hand in his pocket and touches something there. By the weight and the shape of the something, he knows that it is a tiny plastic baby.

'Well,' Miss Mitchelmore says, she is clapping her hands, encouraging the other children to do the same by looking around at them. 'I expect your father is very proud of you, too,' Miss Mitchelmore says, smiling so hard it looks as though her face might crack.

'Now, Jake, do you have your Show and Tell?' she says, looking around again, but Jake is already shuffling to the front of the class, holding the lump under his jacket. Benny sees white fur with pointed little claws on the end of some twisted yellowish toes, ears that are half formed and show the way into the dog's head.

Some of the class scream when Jake drops the lump of dog carelessly on Miss Mitchelmore's desk, in the spot where Benny's fleet of planes had been moments before.

'This one came out dead,' he says.

Benny Dodd
25 Wish Drive
Plum Regis

Dear Paolo,

Thank you for your letter about Sunny Air's actual existence as a Malaysian Restaurant that is not an actual airline. I am sorry that I worried you. I promise that I will not try to come to the restaurant because it is true that I cannot find my father there. Thank you for telling me this news and also for telling me stories about your father, Paolo Snr, and his job as a karate instructor in the army. I have talked to Elaine a lot and I will do what you say and have some karate lessons, which might help me to deal with the boys in my class, although not the teacher, who is still making me come to many Pow-Wow meetings.

I had a very bad time last week, as Jake Standing brought a dead dog into school for Show and Tell. Jake told Miss Mitchelmore that his brother said he should take the dog for scientific purposes, but she was very angry with him, and then when I only tried to say that maybe he shouldn't listen to his brother next time, he became very angry with *me*, taking my painting and tearing it into pieces. This was a painting of my father, John Dodd.

And that same day, when I went home, Elaine was still working, talking to a man on the phone while she was lying in front of the TV, watching a video of Kylie Minogue working out, with the volume turned down to 3. I tell you, Paolo, I wish that I knew some karate already, because I felt almost like I was in front of the train then, and my ears started making a roaring sound. I wasn't crying but a dog was barking outside, very loud, and I could hear Elaine talking and talking explicit material (that's what Miss Mitchelmore calls it), and it was like something snapped, just how you explained it in your letter, although I know that you think it is real bullsh*t to go in front of a train, and it is really bad about your cousin who drives trains and got a mental disease from seeing someone die.

But anyway, I was nearly about to do something really crazy already when I saw one of the cards on the floor by the cupboard under the stairs, where Elaine keeps all the prizes from Deelite (the company that Elaine works for), and I won't describe it, but the woman on the card was in a really explicit material position and she looked like she was laughing at me, not laughing, but smirking, you know. And then I was in the Deelite cupboard; crawling right into it, looking for all the cards I could find and tearing them into tiny little pieces, just like Jake did to my picture.

And Elaine was of course screaming at me in the background, and she actually hung up the phone, even though she always said that it isn't right to hang up on a man because he might go off and kill someone or attack them, but guess what, though, Paolo – guess what I found in the back of the cupboard – you won't believe it! It was a whole plastic bag full of Sunny Air planes! Enough planes for every birthday until I am twenty-five years old at least!

Elaine couldn't explain because she was hiccupping so much from crying, and my brain was trying to spin itself so that I could understand what was going on with the planes, my father, the lying, and the realising that I couldn't go and see my dad at Sunny Air, and this was before you had even written to tell me that Sunny Air is, in real life, a Malaysian restaurant only forty-five miles away from my actual home in Plum Regis.

Elaine said that I didn't understand, which was true, and that she'd been trying to protect me, and I told her that I'd been writing to my father at Sunny Air this whole time, even though a few days later I got your nice letter, Paolo, but at the time I did think your Malaysian restaurant address was where my father, John Dodd, was working as a famous pilot. And Elaine's phone was ringing, probably it was the man who needed to be finished, but she was crying even more, and then she told me the truth, right through her compulsive lies, that my father was still working as a caretaker in the block of flats that we used to live in when I was a tiny baby. He lives in the exact same place we all lived together, can you believe it! And I said, "Well why doesn't he come then, my father?" And Elaine said very seriously that he has his problems, and that's why – nothing to do with me, apparently.

And that's pretty much what you said, Paolo, when your letter came three days later, when I had burnt all of my planes in a horrible-smelling cloud. This was in a park where the sometimes-bad-kids play out; there is a butterish-coloured climbing frame that is low on the ground, like a dog, and this is where I used to sit and watch for Sunny Air planes because the planes fly over there, although now I know that there are no Sunny Air planes and that my father would not be flying in one even if there was one that existed. Jake Standing wasn't there, and the other kids stood away from me while I put firelighter on the planes. Elaine came to the park with me too and kept crying but nodding her head at me, like it was a kind of funeral, and just as the flames were getting really big, I said, very loud, 'And those!' pointing to Elaine's red slippies; and she was so surprised that she *did* put them on the fire.

Elaine had to walk home barefoot!

I said to Elaine that maybe we would be okay together, even though she *is* still a compulsive liar, and because I felt sorry for her mainly. But she hugged me and said that we could get a dessert burger at the Plum Regis department store, which is a burger where everything is made from sweets – the bun is marshmallow, the burger and the lettuce and tomato are made out of brown and green and red gummy stuff, not fully the size of an actual burger, obviously. Elaine's work phone was ringing, that man probably, so she said, 'After this call.' And I just went upstairs and looked at my empty windowsill, thinking about my dad, John Dodd, and how he is not a pilot.

But after that, we did go, and I did eat a dessert burger, and we even had milkshakes: strawberry and chocolate.

So I think that you might be right, that Elaine is maybe more or less okay, although I don't know about what you said about the trying to make ends meet bit, because remember I said about the money in the drawer? But anyway, just in case, do you have any jobs at the Sunny Air restaurant? It was bad to hear about how many hours you have to work and that you don't get paid for your lunch hour, but I would still like a job and, even though I am only ten, I am still mature, as I'm sure you can tell. I would be able to pick things up quickly, and it's really just in case things don't work out with the karate, or if I find out that you were wrong about Elaine. But anyway, thanks for writing back and write again, cos it's very nice to hear from you, and I think we could be pen pals, so I will be waiting to hear back from you. Okay, Paolo?

From your friend,

Benny

Benny is in front of his house. He is wearing one of his Christmas presents, a cheese-coloured cowboy hat with a red ribbon, and the ribbon is blowing in the breeze. It is snowing and Benny is digging to make a big mound, the body of a snowman, or woman. Benny is thinking about going to watch the planes flying over the park on the hill later. The planes always fly over the hill, even on Christmas Day.

While Benny digs, he is panting a little bit and he doesn't realise, but he has dug quite deep, below the surface of the snow, where the mud is. Benny sees the wing of a plane, one that he must have forgotten to collect for his bonfire, and he stops still and looks at it for a while, until he hears his panting echoing back at him. Jake Standing is there; he holds a big tobacco-coloured greyhound on a lead. The dog strains to reach the place where Benny's fence is broken, the two flanks of wood that have dissolved like old cereal in the snow. Jake's mouth is tight and Benny looks from Jake to the dog, back to his house where he can see his mother, cradling the telephone like it is a baby, whispering lovingly into the plastic.

'Happy Christmas Day,' Benny says, while he and Jake look at each other. There is a bruise on Jake's cheekbone and he doesn't have a jacket on, only a light fleece. Underneath the fleece, Benny can see the colour of their school uniform jumper.

'Someone has to walk him,' Jake says, as though Benny has asked him why he is out in the snow, on Christmas Day. Benny shrugs; he doesn't tell Jake about his new Christmas kitten, Baby, her sticky black eyes, and the pale pink beans in the bottom of her paws, how his mother had woken him by placing the kitten very gently on his pillow.

'It's a beautiful dog,' Benny says, although the animal isn't beautiful, he looks miserable and restless; the orangish flank vibrates with the angry beating of his heart. Benny can smell the Christmas lunch that his mother is cooking, while she talks to men on the telephone, lonely men on Christmas Day. There is smoke tingeing the air; some part of the Christmas lunch must be burning.

'Beautiful?' Jake snorts. 'He'd rip your arms and legs off.' He nudges the dog, tries to make him bark. Jake pulls his fleece around himself. He keeps glancing at the warm glow in Benny's front window; there are decorations from Deelite, some plastic Santas and coils of yellow fairy lights. On the windowsill, there is a card from Paolo, inviting Elaine and Benny to the Sunny

Air restaurant sometime in the New Year. The restaurant is quite far away, much further than the boundaries of Plum Regis, further than Upper Skein and the Lilybank River, and even than Clutter, where Benny's father lives; but there will be battered, deep-fried bananas, so he says, and hot peanut butter sauce.

Jake says, half-heartedly: 'Didn't fancy a ride on yer dad's jumbo jet today, then?'

Benny shakes his head. He sees the family next door walking on the other side of the road. The little girl is slightly bigger, longer, and wearing an elf costume underneath a giant pink coat. The family wave at Benny, all smiling, as they always do – they have given him a Christmas book called Aviation Adventures, the mother kissing him on the top of the head and saying, 'Good boy,' as if he was a much younger child.

'No,' Benny says, 'not today.'

Benny can see that Jake doesn't want to move on with his walk; he is struggling to stop his teeth clattering together, clenching his jaw.

Absently, Benny reaches down to pull the plane out of the earth, smoothing the crystals of snow and the mud away from the wings. He is thinking about Jake's brother coming into school to speak to Miss Mitchelmore, after the dead puppy Show and Tell. Jake's brother taking Jake outside, the children running to the window to watch. Benny turns the plane over in his hand.

'Here,' he says, holding it out.

'What's that?' Jake says, although he knows.

Jake is suspicious, not wanting to look at the plane.

'My brother already got me loads of these,' he tells Benny, through his clenched teeth.

'Here,' Benny says again.

Jake shifts the lead from one hand to the other and then he snatches the plane.

'Dog can use it as a toy,' he says, and he walks away, very quickly, towards Benny's special park, on the hill. Benny thinks that he hears Jake saying something in the distance, but the wind steals the words, and he can't be sure.

The Flea-Trap

The white cats have kittens and we lure them into our trap with bits of cheese left over from lunch.

Our bedroom is underground, part of the basement where the caretaker's cleaning equipment is kept, and basically invisible if you are looking at Paradise Block from the outside. There are no other people living inside this underground corridor, only machines that chug and groan, like monsters or strange friends. When we leave our bedroom, there are stairs that reach up to our next floor, an arm grappling towards the amber light, and then a shadowy area with a giant antique mirror, where you say a dark fox lives.

The flat is upside down, then: the cosy upstairs rooms that can be seen from the street are the kitchen and living room, and then there are the two dark underground rooms with just one window, near the ceiling of our bedroom. This window is cracked and broken into two pieces, like the lens of a child's spectacles that have been lost, crushed on the road. This is where the kittens come in, snuffling around at the damp foot of Paradise Block; they drop through space like little furry asteroids.

I don't really *love* the kittens – but you do, and you make them wear the baby's clothes: hats and bibs. You try to put the little shoes on their paws.

We aren't children.

The baby is *our* baby, but as soon as we saw all the things that it can do, the dull solemnness of its very dark gaze, we wished to *put it back*; we wished that a muster of crows might come and take it away. We looked for our play elsewhere, subtly at first, just out of the corners of our eyes, and then abundantly, turning circles in the darkness like drunk dogs or horses galloping on merry-go-rounds. We left Paradise Block, went off even further than The Brass Cross, out into Clutter town centre, where the department store eats up the land and people walk around very quickly, buying things and then staring into the air with glass eyes, clutching their shopping bags like trophies. Nobody looked at us; nobody saw when we paid old people and the homeless to perform tricks with juggling balls and small knives, when we crouched in doorways, telling wild stories and promises to the little children that we sometimes met.

The white kittens are excellent, almost like the baby itself, but more active and amusing. However, because they are feral, the kittens have fleas, and we have to cover ourselves with a cream that repels them, although we still get bitten very thoroughly. I ask you whether we should cover the baby with cream also, a glossy egg, but you say that the baby will be fine; *the dear little baby likes it well enough.*

That's another thing, we sometimes pretend that we are aristocrats as a joke: we say, *The baby will take its tea at four o'clock*, or nowadays, *What shall the kittens partake of for lunch?* This drives us both into hysterics because these characters could not be further from our true selves: *wealthy, outdated, proper*; it reminds us of our families who live miles away from our new home in Paradise Block. We laugh about their quibbles over money and houses, their concerns over our routines – smashed windows; poisoned cousins with scratched and dented bodies; the broken cars and their plucked-out eyes.

Really, we live exactly how we want to – we only ever have fun; we are playful, just like the children that we sometimes befriend, although our occasional companions have described us as *extremely mature*; they gawk up at us, chewing nervously on the ends of their plaited hair.

The only interruption is when Angelique comes around to our place.

Angelique is a half-blind ex-department-store girl. We found her in The Brass Cross, drunk on honey wine and starving, chewing on a slice of lemon and whimpering stories about her lost daughter, 'Pinkie'. Angelique is our childcare now, although you'd think that *we* worked for *her*. She yells at us, and gestures towards where the baby lives, demanding that we take responsibility (you say, *We will not partake in responsibilities*, and we giggle, but Angelique grabs your grandmother's Peking vase and smashes it, scaring us badly).

Even so, when Angelique leaves, mumbling and swaying, bruising her limbs on our heavy furniture, we always go back to the room with the white kittens. We don't mean to; we wish that something could change! We are cowed and we talk about responsibilities all the way down the stairs, you stopping to examine a circle of silverfish bites in the wallpaper, or a tattered comic that some friend has left. But then, when we get to the upside-down landing, at the bottom of the stairs, there are two rooms there: the baby's room, with the baby howling, as blue as a plum, and our room, where the white kittens are mewing gently.

We have to pick the kittens; we just have to!

And we've solved the problem of the fleas.

So there, Angelique!

It was the day when you won £100 at the Plum Regis dog track and jumped down on to the dusty grass to celebrate, making the earth judder. There was frothing pink blood everywhere because the dog had bitten into its own tongue and you had to run, as though imitating the stuffed rabbit that circles the track. We laughed all the way to the train, you shouting, 'The dark fox! I am the dark fox!' and punching the violet air. But then, as we were about to open the folding doors to the station, I gasped, pointed. It was a sign written in terrible handwriting, all across a shadowy shop front:

Itching for a Solution to Vermin Problems?
TRAPS
ALL VERMIN
KILL . THEM . DEAD.

We looked at each other, most suddenly quiet.

The trap looks a lot like a child's carousel, and it lights up with a warm orange glow that lures the fleas when you plug it in.

We close the door and watch the trap, scratching our bites and gazing at the sticky plate where the fleas will be caught.

You are playing with a white kitten, dangling an abandoned rag doll in front of its face, when the first flea lands in the trap.

'Hark!' I say, and you look, giggling, falling down on to your belly and nearly crushing the kitten.

'My God!' you say, removing the yowling scrap of fur. 'A little blighter!'

We stop laughing and watch the flea. It is stuck to the floor of the flea-trap ride with only one small portion of its body, and it desperately wants to escape, wriggling with all its might, and then going still for only a few seconds before it starts again. We are quiet, and I see you thinking, scratching one bite very intently.

'But look what it did to me!' you say, showing me the proof, your giant hive.

'Nobody blames you,' I reply, chewing my lip. The flea tears off one of its legs in its struggle, and it lays there, an eyelash on the plate. 'But it does seem—' I start, and you agree.

'Yes. It is desperately cruel.'

There is some crashing and banging and we realise that Angelique has crawled through our upstairs window-space again. We never answer the buzzer that stings and invades our games, so she does this often, leaving yellow baby formula and mashed banana on the table. We have no idea how she affords such things as we barely ever pay her and she has a rash of moth holes all across the shoulder of her cardigan. I remember once we saw Angelique clinging to the baby and crying, really blubbering, and blowing her nose like a clown's trumpet, singing out, 'Pinkie, oh Pinkie,' over and over. We watched her where we cannot be seen, crouched behind the banister at the mouth of the stairs (where you say the dark fox lives), until she stopped crying and let her hand sneak into the darkness of the larder, pulling out one of the brown bottles that we keep there.

'She's a scoundrel,' you say, and we look at each other, necks very straight and eyes wide, hair pushed back from our foreheads in earnest, until I crack because you have used some of our funny language in such a serious situation. And now everything seems ridiculous again.

We just can't be solemn for long!

We hear Angelique coming down the stairs, into our dark place. She is knocking on the door, but we cannot stop giggling, and it is only when we hear her leaving, the window flapping shut again, that you say, 'We should kill them.' And I agree.

'One by one,' I say. 'We'll make it quick.'

For the rest of the day, and then the night, we lie on our bellies by the trap. The white kittens sleep and eat and cough up little bones, and we stamp on the fleas with the bottoms of pencils the very moment they jump into the trap.

We take it in shifts later. I wake and find you've fallen asleep, your pencil still poised, and I shake you.

There are seven fleas stuck to the trap.

We move around the carousel, stamping bodies with the bloody ends of the pencils, which become like hooves.

The fleas are cinnamon-coloured inside, only a shade lighter than their shells, not like the blood inside ourselves, or inside the baby, which is a very different colour indeed.

This continues for a week or so: you scuttle up and down the stairs, fetching us liquorice and banana chips, jars of jowly maraschino cherries and honey wine from the larder; a pisscup for me because I cannot aim my jet out of the small window that peeks on to the street. The dark fox is sleeping, you say, and I nod wisely, glancing up at the shadowy shape that flashes in the mirror when you leave the room and disappear.

The floor of the flea-trap turns muddy with the amber corpses of the fleas; they cannot resist the radiant carousel, and every day more seem to come.

I see you one morning, talking to yourself in the mirror at the top of the stairs.

'When will they perish?' you are asking, and you stab at the mirror frantically with your staff.

We are calling the murdering pencils 'staffs' now.

Days pass, and I am dulled by the tedium of the fleas – their legs decorating my staff, which I toy this way and that, watching the yellow-eyed kittens scratching in the corners of the room. I stare at the animals for several minutes, their white fur visibly trembling with the energy of fleas, before I suddenly realise something very terrible.

'The kittens—' I start.

'I've been thinking the same,' you say. You are sitting

on the landing outside the room, wrestling with a ring of bites on your neck, your eyes rolling.

When the white kittens are posted out of the small window, they are not able to hunt as they are too young and have been lured away from their mother who might have taught them such things. They have not been trained in any survival skills, nor do they have any natural capabilities, because they are quite malnourished and small, and they seem to glow like luminous white slugs against the blackness outside. We are concerned for their safety, and so we throw morsels of fish out from the window, but inevitably, the larger cats take the lion's share, and we soon forget.

With the kittens banished, you become very depressed, talking to yourself in the mirror often, and I cannot think of anything to cheer you up, so I offer to take you out to the dogs in Plum Regis.

'Yes,' you say, and I leave the bedroom, joining you in the shadowed hallway.

You are talking to the dark fox in the mirror when I realise that Angelique has taken the baby, and you drop your staff in your surprise, turning to me with blazing eyes.

'Our baby!' you say uncertainly.

You charge past the dark fox and into the warm light, and I shout, 'Where are you going?' But when I plunge into the living room, you are just slumped down on the stained sofa. I see your face in the bright orange blaze of our upstairs rooms and it looks very different.

The fleas have indeed been eating us alive.

'Now we have nothing,' you say. 'No white kittens, no baby.'

I sit beside you, neither of us really wanting to watch the dogs racing in Plum Regis, nor to admit that they have become boring. I begin to feel depressed and I keep visualising the mad, bloody-jawed dogs running around and around, never catching anything, never having any real fun.

You take a packet of cigarettes from your dressing-gown pocket and they are all broken and bent, but you put one in your mouth and suck on it wildly until I find a box of matches on the dining-room table, underneath the dirty pile of lost dolls and toys. I notice that there are tubes of paint everywhere, and juvenile drawings of families and pets, pins stuck into the wood. Angelique has taken all of the remaining honey wine from the larder; I wonder whether she will call the baby 'Pinkie', like her lost child, and distractedly thumb some liquorice into my mouth. You sit and smoke and I am beside you, fussing with my staff and feeling bored and depressed, until just then, we hear a sound outside.

You are still smoking while we hide, each behind a red paisley curtain, and I watch through the plume that you blow elegantly from your lips.

There are three children, two girls and a boy, and the girls are playing by throwing a small round stone over the boy's head. The boy looks unhappy, but he stands there just the same, trying to keep very still so as not to upset the girls' aim.

You open the upstairs window-space just a crack, and

we watch them for a little while, speaking to each other only with the glass inside our eyes. You look very dark and handsome, standing in the shadow of the curtain, with the bites decorating your high red cheekbones, and I gaze at you proudly.

Eventually, when the children are nearly bored of the stone game, and the sky has turned from yellow to grey to sooty black, I slink out of the window and on to the gravel in front of Paradise Block; my house-slippers crackle over the fish bones. I am smiling, reaching inside my gown for the sticky slabs of liquorice, always a big hit with the children.

There is a quick exchange. I tell the children, the eldest girl, that we have lost our baby; that we have sweets and kittens inside, a tame fox who laughs and runs in circles, trying to catch his own tail. The girl asks me why my face is burnt all over and I reach up to touch my skin, surprised. I have not realised that, of course, my face has been gnawed at.

'It's a game we play,' I tell her, and the girl cocks her head to one side, drops the stone.

'A game?' she says.

I notice that she has very cramped teeth inside her mouth; her jaw is small, like the jaw of a lamb, and her face is very bony, almost prehistoric-looking. She walks towards the amber light, and the littler girl, who has plaits with bits of ribbon sewn through, clings to her arm, the boy sulkily following the procession, trying to step in the exact footsteps that the girls leave invisibly on the path.

I look at the lights that are shining, warm and orange inside the flat, our carousel, the plate underneath, muddied with bodies, and I see your eyes and teeth sparkling, my dark fox.

Before I follow the children, I stop and pick up the stone that the girl has dropped. It is a very good stone, round and full of character. I put the stone in my dressing-gown pocket.

I smile and think to myself, although I don't tell you, about how my life goes round and round, just like this—

You

Once, I was out at the club, wearing a white dress that was designed to make boys/guys/men feel really hot under the collar and really hard inside their pants.

This was not the kind of dress I would have usually worn, but I had just recently broken up with my fiancé of five years and two months. My fiancé had left me for another woman, one who made him hungry, ravenous for her body and her love, and so I wore the dress.

I thought that I looked good, and I felt powerful, and when I walked in my high heels, it was as though I didn't care about my ex-fiancé, or that delicious-tasting other woman.

So I went into the club, and then I saw You, but after a few seconds You started to talk to someone with extremely large breasts, and I realised that this probably wasn't You at all, but that I was yet to find You. And then I saw that there were many Yous in the club and I thought, *Jesus Christ! Who needs a relationship!* And I began to weave my wicked spell on all the men on the dance floor.

After an hour or so, my friend patted me on the back while I was sick in the toilet. She said that the dress really suited me and that she thought I had lost weight.

She also said that she had always been jealous of my relationship with my mother, who had been dead for more than a year, but who, when we were much younger, teenagers, had always made my friend her own cocktail using vodka and sugar and maraschino cherries, and had let her iron her hair using her straightener. We talked about my friend's relationship with her mother for thirty to forty minutes, and then I realised that there was no time to find You before the lights came on in the club, and I made her come back out of the toilets and into the club and dance to Rihanna even though she was crying. She was crying and singing at the same time and also dancing in a very weird way.

I looked at some magical and impossibly young girls, who were wearing big clothes where only a tiny bit of their bodies showed, like their wrists or sometimes their bellies. These girls were surrounded by ravenous men, and they danced extremely well, sparkling dust motes flying through the air around them, their plastic cups full of pink wine strobing through the light. I tried to dance like them, and I pulled down my white dress, and a man said, 'Put them away, love!'

He was the first man to have spoken to me all night and, even though he was rude and had luminous orange hair, I thought he might be You.

In the taxi queue my friend told me to pull myself together and act my age; I told her to pull *her*self together, but I knew that she was jealous, because I was talking to a man.

'Did yous have a good one?' the man said.

He had a nice jacket and carried a blue plastic bag.

'Oh yeah, it was great,' I said. 'We danced all night.'

'You wanna come back to mine? We can split the taxi fare.'

The man didn't look at me.

I thought, *I'm not going to sleep with You on the first date.* And then I thought: *I'm not actually on a date.* I took off my puffy white jacket even though I was freezing.

'I'm so hot,' I said.

The man looked at all the other women in the queue. My friend was green, like she was going to be sick. There was a bright white light shining over the taxi rank.

'So how about it, then?'

I laughed a bit.

'I'm not that kind of girl, mister!' I said.

I thought that he looked very disappointed, and so I said, 'I'll give you my phone number, though.'

'Why?' he said.

'What do you mean why?'

He shrugged and looked away.

It was while he was looking away, taking out materials to roll a cigarette, that I realised that he certainly could be You and that a chance like this probably wouldn't come round again for a long while.

'Okay!' I said wildly. 'Let's do it!'

My friend was very tired and moaned about safety precautions and said, 'Don't do it, Rose.'

But I did, and when we got in the taxi he huddled up inside of his big jacket and didn't say anything, so I said my address, Flat 17, Paradise Block, Box Close, in the space where he should have said his. My place was fairly close anyway.

He didn't say anything else the whole rest of the journey either, even though I tried to start several conversations, and I ended up talking to the taxi driver, who I started to realise might be You instead.

I almost asked the taxi driver for his phone number and I said, 'Can I get a receipt?' but in a low voice, as if to say, *Can I have your phone number?* And while he was writing it out, I held my breath, and then ran on to the concrete stairwell to activate the lights and see if he had written his phone number on the bottom.

He hadn't, though.

The man sat silently on my sofa while I showed him my favourite china animals, passed to me from my mother, and he took three dark brown bottles out of his blue plastic bag, and still wouldn't really make any conversation after he had drunk them all, so I just put on the radio really loudly.

Later, when I took off my white dress, he tried to get an erection, but he couldn't.

I realised that he wasn't You.

Timespeak

On Thursdays, Mr Grisco would come right to my door to deliver my groceries. He didn't mind coming because his shop was just across from where Elaine worked, which was actually just across from Paradise Block, alongside The Brass Cross, further than the car park and the bus stop, but not that far, really, not for a businessman, like Mr Grisco. In those days, the view was just noise and aggravation, but later, when everything became quiet, these dulled lights and discarded buildings were interesting to me, like smudged visions from a memory; no, like visions from a peculiar dream.

Mr Grisco put the shopping bag down and walked over to my television, turned the television off. He told me that I have the television very loud, too loud; he does not like to shout over the television.

'You are not very sociable, Mr Cornflower,' Mr Grisco scolded, but then, straight away pleased again: 'However! You are my most regular customer. Fifteen years, and you've never even changed your order. It is a wonderful thing for a businessman, Mr Cornflower, when the businessman can rely on his customers.'

Mr Grisco paused to dab his lip with a handkerchief, one that was matching in colour to the crisp shirt that he liked to wear. He always dressed very well, Mr Grisco. The shopkeeper never sat down to drink his tea or to eat the White Fingers biscuits that I always laid out for him, but he often stayed for long enough to perform these speeches for me, or for himself – I think that these lectures were a kind of therapy for him. I watched Mr Grisco's mouth to see if he would say anything else; my hearing was already very bad, so I often resorted to lip-reading, even then, and when his mouth didn't open again, I said, 'Well now.' And I asked him politely, 'Would you like one of these biscuits, Mr Grisco?'

Mr Grisco continued, as if he hadn't heard me.

'There was a time, Mr Cornflower, when people really cared about each other. They would all know each other a certain amount and they would say "hello". People would always be leaving their doors unlocked, their possessions on the ground outside ...' Mr Grisco trailed off, as though he had forgotten what he was going to say. Even though I could not hear everything, this particular conversation was so familiar to me that I almost prompted him to continue. I knew that Mr Grisco had lived in Clutter for more than thirty-five years, but I never remembered such a time; I don't remember what it was like to leave my door unlocked, to say hello to anyone in the street or on the bus. My ears were ringing again, and I wanted the conversation to come to its natural conclusion so that I could continue concentrating on blocking out the buzzing, the whirring and the clicking.

'You see the billboard, Mr Cornflower?'

Mr Grisco pointed to the window, and I squinted at the scene outside, as though I had never noticed the big department-store billboard before. He held a can of macaroni thoughtfully against the window-light.

'The Clutter department store,' said Mr Grisco, 'they take my customers. No businessman can compete. They will take this can of macaroni, good macaroni I sell, they sell bad macaroni for twenty pence cheaper and the customers, they go, they don't give a damn about my macaroni.'

Mr Grisco crashed the tin down hard on the kitchenette counter and a pile of Timespeak brochures leapt into the air, scattered across the work surface. He hadn't performed like this before, so I was surprised, and although I have never been afraid of Mr Grisco, I shuffled backwards, pressed my body into the crevice next to the fridge. One of my slippers had come off. The veins in my foot were blue-green and the toenails were long. Mr Grisco and I stared at my foot, and I was ashamed; my old and disfigured foot was an object from a world that Mr Grisco, the successful businessman, could not understand. The silence was very close, but even so, it was like a fairground of noise inside my ears.

'You thinking of being a customer to the Clutter department store, Mr Cornflower?'

Mr Grisco looked at me, straight in my face.

I said, 'No, no, Mr Grisco. I will never give my custom to anyone but you.'

He nodded approvingly, seemingly calmed, and I touched my crisp hairline. My heart was beating very fast and my ears had started to really scream now. I felt the noise build as different sounds began to slot into the black silence.

'Mr Grisco?' I called after him as he strode down the thin corridor.

I thought that I might say, *It is like we have become friends, over the years*, but of course, I didn't.

'Yes, Mr Cornflower?'

I stood on the metal line between the grey of my carpet and the dead blue of the carpet in the hallway outside. This was as far as I ever went, as close as I ever came to leaving my little flat.

'What's the problem, Mr Cornflower?' he shouted.

'Well now,' I started, but Mr Grisco was far away; he didn't want to walk any closer, and the very bright electric light in the corridor was hurting my eyes. I saw the way Mr Grisco was standing, so full of purpose, so ready to move on to his next customer, to discuss the wrongdoings of the Clutter department store in some other flat.

And then, 'Nothing, Mr Grisco.'

Mr Grisco nodded and walked away, to the stairwell, which led to where the world was.

I turned on my lamp: click. I looked out of the window to where the big Clutter department-store billboard stood. 'Open 24 hours,' the red letters shouted.

I heated the macaroni in my small saucepan and looked at the three White Fingers on the china plate.

It was still twenty hours until Elaine's next call.

*

When the telephone rang it was only 1.30 p.m.

I walked to the kitchenette and flicked down the kettle switch.

The kettle spat at me.

The kettle was broken.

The sound of the broken kettle did not drown out the sound of the telephone ringing.

Maybe she has changed her shift, I thought.

I put my hands over my ears; I felt the blood in the thick fleshy bit at the bottom. The ringing of the telephone made different sharp sounds swell out of nothingness in my head. I turned the television off and pushed the phone into my ear, very hard.

'Hello, Mr Cornflower, this is Elaine from Timespeak Funeral Planners, devising a vision of your afterlife. Have you ever thought about how your loved ones are going to cope after you are unfortunately dead?'

Elaine was reading from her script.

'I don't know, Elaine,' I said. Her voice was moving further away and then closer, like a rush of soft wind.

I touched the kettle with my forefinger; it was so hot.

Silence.

'Elaine?'

'Yes.'

'Did you change your shift?'

'Yes.'

'Well now,' I said.

I thought about what to say.

And then, 'Do you leave your doors unlocked ever, Elaine? Mr Grisco says that people used to leave their doors unlocked all the time, because of trust and community.'

Silence.

I waited for a beat or two; sounds crammed into my ears, and I had to really strain to find where her voice might slot into the mess. Somewhere in reality I could hear another voice, Elaine's team manager, Tanya, reminding her staff about their targets for the week.

'Hello?' I asked.

'Hello,' said Elaine.

'The sky is a very beautiful shade of blue today, isn't it, Elaine?'

I looked across the fringe of soggy grass and wet concrete, the big, bare trees, all the way past the car park and the bus stop, to the building where Elaine worked, its orange plastic roof, the long grey body surrounded by pale blue, sulphur-yellow tints to the clouds. 'TIMESPEAK: A Slice of Heaven.' Mr Grisco's little shop was there too, half boarded up, as though a pale brown snake was trying to eat it whole; I could just about see the bright red signs in the exposed windows, there was a big sale on.

Elaine was clearing her throat.

'It looks like there is sunshine in the clouds today, Elaine,' I said.

'Yes,' said Elaine.

'Yes?' I said.

I held my breath.

'Did you receive your brochure this week, Mr Cornflower?'

'Yes, actually, I received it yesterday.'

A pink cough flew out of my mouth and left a thread of mucus on my palm. My voice sounded like it belonged to somebody else and my ears were crackling. I knew that

Tanya listened back to the calls, that there was a sanction for not sticking to the script; I couldn't ask too much of Elaine.

Silence.

'Did your results come in?' Elaine was whispering.

'Yes they did, the doctor said that they were quite positive, although my hearing is getting worse. I think I'll lose it altogether pretty soon. I have this ringing in my ears and ...' I paused, worried that I would upset Elaine. 'Never mind,' I said, and I put a happier tone into my voice: 'The doctor is from Pakistan, you remember? He is a very nice gentleman called Omar. A Pakistani gentleman called Omar Sharpe. He visits me at my home, comes right to the front door.'

'Yes?' said Elaine, speaking at full volume again now. 'Have you considered a biodegradable coffin, Mr Cornflower?'

'Well now, I wouldn't rule it out, Elaine,' I said.

I looked at the naked tree outside, the tulips that had been stamped into the mud. My eardrums began to throb and I sighed.

'Do you want me to get back to you on that one?' she was quiet again, and I had to let the words make impressions on my brain, Tanya shouting in the background. Timespeak sales staff were supposed to close deals, slam the lid down – bang! When Elaine first started calling she would go in on me very hard: on one occasion I had already given her half of my account details, the long queue of silver numbers on the front of my bank card, and then the line went dead. She must have known that we would be friends, even then.

'Yes please, Elaine. I'll have a think about it.'

'Okay, Mr Cornflower, you have a nice day.'

'Can I expect you at this time now, Elaine?'

'Yes, I've changed my shift, Mr Cornflower. I'm taking a class ...'

'A class?'

Elaine cleared her throat again.

'Thank you for your time, Mr Cornflower. Have a lovely afternoon.'

'I'm always here, Elaine. Always here to chat, if you need a friend.'

Silence.

And then Elaine's short breaths, the jangling dialling tone.

I folded the pillow around my head. My ears were much worse at night-time and the teenagers outside would not stop fighting in the car park. The lights, blue-white, hazy, the lights would not stop shining through any small crack between my curtains. I'd sometimes taped the material to the frame at night-time, but they always came unstuck and sneaked open, just a touch. At 3 a.m. a stone or something similar hit my window and my heart began to beat horribly quickly under my breast. Inside my eardrums everything was a whir of noise, like strange space signals and radio frequencies. Burglar alarms jangled through the empty hallways of Paradise Block.

At 1.25 p.m. the next day I switched *Countdown* off and sat waiting. The presenters had been talking over each other and the contestants seemed insane, mumbling into their jumpers and ignoring the questions.

I turned my lamp on: click.

It was a dark grey day and the lamp cast a circle of light over and around my chair. The fuse twitched inside the thin glass, like an almost dead fly. When the telephone rang I could see the shadow of my arm reaching out and lifting the receiver.

'Hello,' I said.

'Hello, is that Mr Cornflower?'

'Of course it is, Elaine,' I said.

'Have you thought about whether you would like to be buried or cremated?'

'We've been through this, Elaine.'

'Oh, yes, of course.'

'I'm sorry; I didn't mean to be rude. That's the last thing I want. It's just ...'

'I can see on your file here, Mr Cornflower, that you were leaning more towards the burial plan over the last few years ...'

'Elaine.'

'Yes, Mr Cornflower?'

'I'm sorry.'

Silence.

'I took the boy out after school yesterday,' she whispered. 'We went to the Plum Regis department store and he had ice cream with red sauce.'

'Benny. He is a lovely boy,' I told her, and then, 'How is he getting on at school now? Does he still want to be an aeroplane pilot?'

Elaine was quiet again. I thought she would go back to her script. Tanya passing like a shark behind her desk.

'Do you ever go outside, Mr Cornflower? Don't you have any friends?'

Silence. My howling ears.

'Well now,' I said.

I could hear bottles smashing on the street, a man's voice: 'Give me that!'

And then, 'I'm afraid.'

Silence.

'We're friends, Elaine,' I told her.

'Yes,' said Elaine.

Then it was the weekend.

Elaine does not go to work at the weekend.

I swallowed my medication, two at a time with great big gulps of skimmed milk, thin and hazy. The smallest pill, the pale green one, it always makes me shake. I pedalled the dial on my hearing aid for a few minutes, dialling reality in and out, always accompanied by the angry shriek of tinnitus. A skip had appeared outside Mr Grisco's shop, and a yellow digger sat next to it, a scorpion guarding a black hole.

I sat in my chair and flicked through a Timespeak brochure. My hands bothered the pages with tremors.

Timespeak Traditional, Timespeak Tiki-Teak, Time-speak Timber and Timespeak Turf.

The brochure was coloured brightly, with young women on each page standing next to the coffins, sitting on the lids or balanced on the edges. One woman was even *inside* a coffin; she was beaming and had one long leg raised, bare feet and toes pointed. It was intimate to see someone's feet; that's what I always felt. Feet could be so different, although we imagine them as pretty much exactly the same. I remembered my mother's feet, the way her toes were squared off straight, like loaves of bread, how she kept her toenails bright red and I never saw what was underneath, even though I was her son.

I thought about the feet of all the people waiting for their next call from Timespeak, strobing through the light underneath thousands of closed doors. The Timespeak database: the files containing the names and addresses of all the people who might be alone or lonely or thinking about death. I wondered if there was a chance that Elaine herself could be on that huge database; did Elaine have red toenails?

I looked at the blur of grey and blue people, bunched up in their coats in the car park outside. It was raining hard.

Maybe one day, when Elaine is between shifts, she will walk out of the bathroom, wet footprints on the lino. She'll lift the receiver and say, just casually, not even imagining who it could be, 'Hello?'

The caller would explode into the safety of her home, Benny oblivious in front of the television, Baby, the white cat, yawning and twisting and stretching in front of the electric fire. 'Hello, Elaine, have you ever thought about personalising your urn? Have you considered a woodland burial? You can have your body turned into a diamond and passed on to a loved— On to, er ... well, maybe not the diamond option, although we *do* have clients who choose to be turned into a diamond and then buried, *as the diamond*, in a personalised urn. Yep, that is actually quite a popular option, Elaine. Elaine? Are you there, Elaine?'

She would drop the telephone in surprise.

Age is like that, Elaine. Always a surprise.

I turned on my lamp: click.

I ate my macaroni. I could still hear the sound of Mr and Mrs Dimorier's television next door; there was still shouting in the street. Who are they, who are they, who are *you*, Elaine?

Do you remember when you said, in the very earliest hours of the day, when I might still have been asleep, 'Have you ever considered, Mr Cornflower, not dying at all, but coming out of your little flat and visiting the fair with Benny and me? Seeing the lights flashing and hearing the laughter, letting the almost-invisible candyfloss dissolve on your tongue?'

I remember what I said, I said, 'Yes.'

And it was true, I had *considered* it; but it was so hard to make the first step all alone, and only the monotonous sound of fear thumped through my ears, right to where my brain slept.

On Monday morning I came downstairs and hung clean underpants and a striped shirt over the hob, attaching them with pegs to the extractor fan. Then I sat and watched them drying, waiting for the sun to rise so that I could turn off my lamp.

At 7.45 a.m. another brochure from Timespeak was shoved under the door, but I didn't even get up out of my chair to add it to the pile. It bothered me on the mat but the crisp parts of my shirt beginning to lift off the grill, the dry patches curling and unsticking, fixated me, and I stared at the living shirt like I was a little boy again.

It was sometime before 10 a.m. that I heard banging at number 3, the door right next to my own, and I wondered:

Who could that be? Because nobody ever bangs on the Dimoriers' door. My thoughts started to scuttle along very quickly. I thought someone or some*thing* has infected Paradise Block, like a handful of lice.

I turned the volume on the television up but it kept on and on, bang, bang, bang. I found myself with my buzzing ear against the smooth chipboard.

It was a young man's voice.

'Hello, are you Mr Dimorier? I'm Jim from Timespeak; we've spoken on the telephone.'

I spread my hand across the chipboard, the grumble of Mr Dimorier's voice; my ears were getting worse every day, so I can't really have heard this, but I imagined I could make out the very faint sound of his scuffling slippers as he adjusted his weight. How had Jim found his way into Paradise Block? Timespeak didn't allow home visits. Jim could be fired if he breached the data protection, if he crossed the line. Tanya was sure to find out. *Elaine is taking a class*, my mind whispered; *you'll never see the lights, taste the candyfloss*. There was the eternal whizzing and fizzing inside my ear.

'I've come to congratulate you on your decision, for the Timespeak Triple Willow. It's fully furnished, isn't it? Yes, look, it's beautiful.'

I strained to hear what Mr Dimorier was saying, but he seemed to be getting closer and then further away.

'Mr Dimorier, we like to come and congratulate all of our customers in person. Timespeak just want to say *well done*,' Jim said warmly.

Mr Dimorier must've stepped outside of his door, because I heard him clearly for the first time.

'Thank you,' he said, 'it's great to see you, Jim. It's, well, it's good to meet you, face to face.'

Mr Dimorier sounded embarrassed, excited and embarrassed, but I didn't wait to hear any more. I pulled my shirt from the fan. It was still wet in parts, but I buttoned it over my vest anyway. The shirt clung to my stomach. I did up my top button, a small smile creeping over my old skin.

The pile of Timespeak letters: crumpled and tea-stained brown-white like rotten stones. Hundreds must've been pushed under my door since Elaine had started calling me. I picked up the whole stack and opened my pedal bin with my foot. I dropped the letters into the bin. I sat in my chair and flicked through the channels, there were horses running frantically around a track, but my thoughts were too fast to properly absorb the pictures, the shouting of the inane commentator. I got up and went upstairs to the bathroom, only to find that I didn't need to urinate. I stood by the little mirror and looked at myself for several seconds.

'Well now,' I said.

When the telephone rang at 9.45 a.m., I answered it very quickly, my hand nearly slapping the cradle on to the floor, not realising, in my excited delirium, that Elaine wasn't due to call for several hours.

'I would like the Cornflower-Blue Timespeak Treble-Breasted Coffin. I would like to order it today, please come and congratulate me. Please come, come and tell me I did the right thing.'

'Certainly, sir.'

Silence.

'Elaine?'

'No, this is not Elaine calling I'm afraid, sir, but I can tell you that you *have* made an excellent decision. If you could just give me the first part of your account number, I can get this life-changing purchase started ...'

'Where is Elaine?' I said, my dry tongue diving from the roof of my mouth.

'Elaine has left us at Timespeak, I'm afraid. She was taking a *class*. Mmmmm. But don't worry, sir; I'll look after you. Anytime you need anything you can ask your Janie; that's my name, Janie Hall. That's okay, isn't it?'

'How can I contact Elaine?'

'I'm sorry, Mr Cornflower, I can't give out Elaine's information. It's against our policy, the data protection. I'm sure if she wants to contact you she will.'

I gave Janie Hall my account details; the silver numbers, listening to her strange voice rise and fall as she repeated them back to me.

'Will you call here any more, Janie Hall?'

'No, I don't think so, Mr Cornflower. I think you're all set, all ready to go.'

Janie cleared her throat awkwardly.

'Goodbye, Janie Hall,' I said.

'Goodbye,' said Janie Hall.

I sat in my chair. I rubbed my hands over my ears and closed my eyes. Outside I could hear girls and boys squealing as they played a game – *come out, come out wherever you are!* – but the sounds throbbed, like waves, an ice-cream van was singing, '...the teddy bears have their picnic', louder, then quieter, and accompanied by an endless screeching, a long slow throb.

When I couldn't hear the television over my roaring

ears, I stared out of the kitchenette window and thought for a moment about each person on the concrete outside. I imagined them turning around and looking up at me, the impossibility of them seeing my pain. A girl was taking eggs from a long green punnet and throwing them methodically against a tree, a small boy in checked shorts darting around in front of her, sometimes yolk and jelly hitting him, running down his arms and legs. The voices of the children shook and clanged and wound aluminium through the loose nerves in my gums, the screeching getting louder. My eyes began to weep. Across the concrete, a teenage girl with strawberry-red hair pushed a pram back and forth; a baby screamed and screamed, and she shouted, 'Fucking hell.'

Behind my temples blood pulsed and I watched as a woman walked up to the front of Paradise Block. The woman had shiny tights on and carried a clipboard, and even though it couldn't have been, something about the way she walked made me think, *Janie*, that's probably Janie Hall, coming to congratulate me on my death. And I looked back into my little room where three White Fingers biscuits lay hardened on the work surface and where the television was a low rustle of rage, voices covering each other, mounting like layers and layers of squabbling chickens, all screeching amongst the throng of evil white noise.

Soon there would be no more screeching, no more television, no more telephone calls with Elaine from Timespeak.

Dr Omar came and briefly placed his hand on mine. He left me a long letter about my deafness and I read it as though it was a letter from a friend who was away on holiday, in Pakistan.

Mr Cornflower, it started.

There is no known treatment for this kind of hearing loss (what tropical disease is this!)

(...) *But life can still continue* (adventures and such tales)

(...) *We recommend support groups* (sharing mint tea and baklava cake)

(...) *Friends and relatives can struggle during this time* (I would write Elaine postcards, pictures of sunsets, a little note for Benny – Wish You Were Here).

I looked at the silent telephone.

It was a Thursday, so I left a note on the door for Mr Grisco: 'Please post this note under door when you come with macaroni order.'

I turned my chair and waited.

When the note came, I opened the door slowly, and Mr Grisco pushed past me, looking angry. I could see that his mouth was moving fast. I wondered if he was talking about the Clutter department store.

I wrote: 'I am deaf.'

Mr Grisco snatched the pen and wrote: 'You are old.'

He handed me the pen back.

'Yes,' I wrote, then, 'that's life.'

Mr Grisco nodded, but he still looked angry.

'You haven't done post,' he wrote.

When he had finished he pointed at the pile of post, and then he stared over my shoulder and out of the window, at the big department-store billboard, and his little shop. The shop was completely boarded up, eaten alive.

73

I looked at the clock and at the post. It was 5.30 p.m. and there were six letters on the mat.

I nodded as he handed me the letters, one with 'CONGRATULATIONS!' printed across its front in huge red letters, and then smaller, 'You're all ready to go.' I put my hand out for the paper, but Mr Grisco pushed me out of the way, marching towards the telephone with his eyes set.

I watched his mouth moving, but I couldn't see the words, and it wasn't long before he slammed the receiver back down.

Mr Grisco began unloading the contents of the brown bags into my cupboards very quickly, jostling cans and cartons.

I scribbled quickly on to the pad and held it up to him. 'ELAINE?'

Then: 'HELP ME'.

Mr Grisco was cruel; this is what he wrote: 'Elaine was trying to sell things.'

Then, in an angry scrawl: 'BUSINESSWOMAN'.

Mr Grisco was too busy, unpacking my groceries very fast, so that he could leave, and I couldn't tell him about the threads between the script: Benny's laryngitis; the bills with the red tops; the spiteful exercise tapes Elaine ordered; how she drank vindictive pink wine, the kind that gave you a brief, raging drunkenness and then a crash of rosy hot misery; when she would go and visit the Lilybank River, pretending to be doing something positive and making healthy choices, but actually just imagining throwing herself into the river where the brown ducks paddled and the ribs of a trolley stuck out of the water, lying there pathetic and not dead, but somehow feeling a release as the water ran over her. And how she had to wear crappy clothes and plastic shoes every day because there was no money, how Benny was ashamed of her, how she never wanted to turn up at the school because she knew he'd be embarrassed, and she didn't want that, but she also didn't want for Benny to think she didn't care, or that his schoolwork wasn't important to her; and how she'd said that I was a good listener, a very good friend to her, even to little Benny.

Mr Grisco wouldn't give me the pen; he wouldn't look into my eyes.

I stood on the metal line between the grey of my carpet and the dead blue of the carpet in the hallway outside. This was as far as I ever went, as close as I came to leaving my flat.

I saw the shopkeeper walk all the way down the corridor, his arms and legs straight with purpose.

I sat in my chair, in the circle of light that my lamp cast.

I watched the different people in their lives on the television. I thought about the people I could have met in Mr Grisco's shop, Mr and Mrs Dimorier sitting in their chairs in flat 3, with just a thin wall between us: I could walk a few steps down the corridor and put my hand on their chipboard front door. I thought about rivers and ducks; bright, happy lights; popcorn kernels bouncing into white clouds; train journeys; balloons, the shape of animals, dolphins, lions, unicorns; exercise classes; snow that might have melted on my head, even the rain that could've soaked through my jacket and washed my body clean.

I wondered if there was fighting going on outside, whether children were playing, babies were crying, dogs were barking, but most of all, I wondered whether my telephone was ringing.

Everything was quiet and empty, but Mr Grisco began to visit me very often, not just on Thursdays, and he was always bringing me something, a small delivery of some kind. I would write him a cheque, pay him for whatever he arrived with, and it was like things were going on, just as normal. There were tins of macaroni, of course, half-pints of skimmed milk, some White Fingers biscuits, but the packets were all grubby, and I wondered where he was storing his goods. For his other work, Mr Grisco went into the town centre to sell things to people who looked at him, always suspicious, now that there was no shop to house him. He never asked to stay the night, but he began to order items to my flat as if he lived there, and sometimes I had to sign invoices, asking the angry delivery men to come right to the door. There was a crate full of umbrellas, 'TOWN OF CLUTTER' printed on their spokes. Mr Grisco told me that he prayed for rain, and if storm clouds gathered outside, he rushed out with an armful of umbrellas, going to bother people, telling them about how awful it is to get wet. Mr Grisco was still a very good businessman, but he looked shabbier, and I pleased him by letting him have some of my smart shirts and even an old suit jacket.

I wasn't much company, but Mr Grisco didn't seem to mind my mood, or that I couldn't hear him. He wrote me notes; we had a yellow notebook that he christened

The Grisco–Cornflower Charter, but he often snatched the Charter back to write something else before I had finished my reply. My handwriting really hasn't changed much since I was a young man, and I was always surprised to see it there, a fingerprint from another life. This made me slow. Usually I was writing something about Elaine, trying to ask Mr Grisco in many different ways about whether the telephone had rung or was ringing; *what were the messages behind the red numbers that flashed on the little black screen*; and Mr Grisco always seemed to think of something else that he wanted to say before I had written barely anything at all.

When it got a little warmer, Mr Grisco would take off his shoes, and I saw his feet, incredibly long and narrow toes that looked like they must have been rolled up and into his shoes. We watched a sad film, and a combination of Mr Grisco's feet, balanced delicately on the edge of my coffee table, and the heroine, lost on a train platform, looking frantically this way and that, made tears come into my eyes. Mr Grisco was snoozing; he was often exhausted when he came to see me, as if he had been awake all night, but he must've heard me snivelling, and when he noticed my wet eyes he stormed out of the flat, jamming his sockless feet back into his loafers, as though he was taking away a treat. He came back much later, it was nearly night-time, with some crushed biscuits and a new carton of milk and he wrote, 'We are OKAY' on the Charter, by that point covered with many words, and then the pen hovered over the yellow page for a few moments before Mr Grisco carefully drew a smiley face underneath the words.

We settled back into our chairs, Mr Grisco making us

both a cup of tea, putting the biscuits out and pulling the table close so that we could reach for them. I began to feel sleepy myself, but it wasn't very much later at all that Mr Grisco leapt out of his snooze again and made me upset my lukewarm tea on my lap. He stumbled across the room, holding his hand out to me, gesturing for me to stay where I was sitting. Then Mr Grisco was talking to someone on the telephone. I sat straight in my chair, the tea soaking through my trouser leg. Mr Grisco became very secretive; he turned his back so that I couldn't read his lips, and then he marched away with the telephone, pulling it from its little table. When I pressed him, exasperated, scrawling 'WHO' on the Charter, he snatched it from my hands, and he wrote: 'Doing business'. And afterwards, Mr Grisco went to the kitchenette to heat some macaroni, offering me a bowl that he had sprinkled with a spice, making the macaroni tubes softly pink. Mr Grisco grinned and presented this dish like it was a grand prize that I had won, and then he got the hairdryer, plugged it in and pointed it at the wet patch on my trousers.

We ate together in the dark; Mr Grisco didn't switch on the television, and I did not turn on my lamp, but he was fidgety, and before we had finished our macaroni, he was up and out of his chair again. He went to the door, opening it just a crack. Mr Grisco was slight, even wearing the bulky suit jacket I had given him, but he stood in front of the figure there, so that I could just see the lower half of a woman, the knees, the shiny tights, and the bottom of a green skirt, some red plastic shoes.

I turned on my lamp, but the click was lost, silenced.

I stood up, and I walked towards the open door.

Hungry

She was eating something, but I couldn't see what it was because her hand was big, and she was wearing strange gloves that matched the colour of her skin exactly. The gloves were very bulky and stiff, and it seemed like she couldn't bend her fingers to pick at her food. She had to pour whatever was in the polystyrene box into the centre of the glove, and then feed from the glove like a cow or a pig. Her head was down but her eyes were watching me. In the bright white light of the food court her eyes were like two black pins; they jabbed right through my big leather jacket, all the way to the underneath of my clothes.

My mother was cutting her burger with a red plastic knife. She kept sanitising her hands with a little bottle that she kept in her bag.

My mother was flattening her burger, squashing it on to the red tray, and then, when she was ready, she picked up a very small cube of burger and held it up to the light, as though she was worshipping the glory of the burger. She put the cube near her nose and sniffed it deeply.

'There,' she said luxuriously. My mother looked at me, spokes of wrinkles shooting out around her lips. She wore her favourite brooch, two sparkling cherries, on the collar of her coat. 'Isn't the food *divine*?' she said. She took out the sanitiser again and wriggled the sharp-smelling wetness around in her hands.

The girl was still staring, tirelessly feeding, her tongue collecting bits of beige and green and red. All of the other girls and women were sitting around, talking on their telephones, twirling bits of their hair, or laughing with their friends, none of them were eating very much of whatever they had in front of them, on their red lunch trays; but this girl kept on and on feeding, dabbing with her tongue. I tried not to look but my eyes kept dragging over to where she sat, and my mother said, 'Oh! Look who has a little crush!'

She waved at the girl with the gloves, gesturing with her glistening hand and smiling.

When we got into the car, my mother was giggly; she said that she had forgotten to go to the toilet. She needed to run back inside.

'How could you forget that you needed the toilet?' I asked her, but my mother was already getting back out of the car and running in her little heels to the place where the Clutter department-store doors were. My mother was quite old but she barely ate anything at all, so her arms and legs looked like they belonged to a child, and then attached strangely to a real mother's head.

I fixed my stare on the automatic doors and dared the girl with the black eyes and the gloves to come outside, into the car park, but she did not appear. She must still have been feeding from her hand in the food court; she had seemed unendingly hungry. I took my eyes away from the door, and looked at my watch instead – the watch had black and silver diamonds around its face, rather than numbers. When my mother returned, three minutes later, she was all pink, and she was wearing a clever, girlish expression on her face.

'Did you enjoy your burger?' Aunt Min shouted. My aunt was much older than my mother, maybe even fifteen years, and her eyes were bugged, grey-blue with cataracts.

Aunt Min had problems with her legs and she was limping around pleasantly and straightening things, a glass frieze of a girl and a boy skating across a lake, pictures of my recently dead Uncle Louie and my fat-headed cousin, Crispin. Her flat had started to fill more and more with rubbish, ever since Uncle Louie had died; but she kept little sections of her space in pristine order. She began to reorganise a bowl of Quality Street that she kept on top of the television, counting the sweets back into the bowl by their colours. As far as I knew, those same Quality Street sweets had been in that bowl for more than ten years, lined up like this: pink, orange, purple, green and blue.

'What would we like to eat, hmm?' Aunt Min yelped, her filmy eyes leaking on one side.

'I'm not hungry,' I reminded Aunt Min. 'I've just had a big burger at the Clutter department store.'

My aunt worked in the Stockings department at the store and she sometimes liked to tell stories about foods or burgers that she said she had eaten over the years, in the distant past, but now she appeared not to hear me. Her hands were still trembling over the bowl of Quality Street, as though she had become stuck there.

'Oh, I could go for pizza,' said my mother, and she chided me gently, 'You're a growing boy. Have just a little bit of pizza.' She was on one of my aunt's huge grey couches, almost submerged beneath the twenty or so embroidered cushions and the stuffed toys that surrounded her, and a small, yellow-eared dog was writhing around at her feet. I knew this dog to be called 'Missy'.

My aunt limped into the kitchen.

'OMELETTE,' she shouted, and she began crashing pans out of the cupboards.

I looked at little Missy, her papery pink tongue. The tongue was very dry and it had chalky white lines of saliva on it.

I was feeling relatively safe on my sofa, wondering, in my head, whether my aunt ever fed the dog, or whether it survived by eating bugs and other small things. It was pleasant, watching Missy's emaciated body writhing and listening to Aunt Min shouting to herself in the kitchen, but when the dog opened her eyes they were very black, and I got a horrible surprise.

'What is it, darling?' my mother said drowsily. She had kicked off her shoes and she was yawning. As I watched, Missy began to lick my mother's ankles and chew on the end of her stocking.

'That tickles,' my mother said.

At the dinner table, my aunt asked, 'Does anybody want to say grace?' and before anyone could answer, she shouted, 'THANK YOU, JESUS.'

I went to pick up my fork but my mother gripped my hand. There was a noise in the hallway and Aunt Min held her head on one side, concentrating on the sound; she brushed her hair away from her ear. My aunt had an agonised expression on her face.

'Jesus?' she said.

Then my mother and my aunt began eating. They made many pleasure sounds as they ground the omelettes into their plates with their forks and Aunt Min kept jumping up to move things around in the kitchen, to turn on the radio and then to turn it off; when she sat down again, she began to chatter about what she was going to make for dinner, and then for the bedtime snack. After a while, I saw that my mother was painting her lips with the yellow paste that she had made underneath her fork.

Missy came into the room and looked up at the table hungrily, her malnourished tongue hanging down like an old sock, and then the buzzer went.

Aunt Min got up from the table very quickly. I heard her shouting to somebody outside, at the front of Paradise Block. She couldn't seem to find out who it was and what they wanted, so she kept coming back down the corridor and into the kitchen and looking at us. My mother dabbed her yellow lips clean with a napkin and went out to the door.

I heard my mother. 'Oh!' she said, and then, giggling, 'Oh! Look who has a little crush!'

My aunt came back into the room and took my shoulders;

I was still wearing my leather jacket, but I could feel her fingers pushing into my flesh. Her eyes were orgasmic in their bulging.

'There's a girl here to see you,' she shouted. 'Do you want to go out for something to eat?'

'I've just had a big omelette,' I said, and I writhed around a bit under Aunt Min's yellow hands, until she had steered me to the door, and I felt the black eyes looking at me, jabbing me. The girl was still wearing the gloves, but she had taken off her jumper and now I could see that her arms were muscular and that she wore a pink dress with white, foamy lace around the neck, and her breasts squashed down inside like two flattened meats.

'Are you hungry?' the girl asked me. She grinned and said that her name was a colour, 'Pinkie', and I just nodded.

I looked at the three smiling females: my mother, Aunt Min and Pinkie. I had to admit that I was: I was very, very hungry.

Ball

John had bought a blue ball for Benny and was bouncing it up against his bedroom wall. He was very excited to see Benny, and the bouncing of the ball was adding to the feeling, making him imagine almost like he *was* Benny, a freckled little boy, bouncing his ball and waiting for *his* father. It wasn't often that John felt this way, what with a whole tower block to maintain, and with his having to work 24/7 to pay Elaine what she wanted in child money, and he decided to take a very small nip of whisky from a new, special bottle, that he'd been saving for an occasion just like this one.

John was strict, steadying himself; he knew that Elaine wouldn't let Benny out to meet him at the station if he didn't get into Plum Regis before it got dark. But John had already packed his bag, and he was almost ready to go. He just had to put his trainers on and grab his jacket, and he could do that in five seconds. John was catching the ball with one hand now, so that he could hold the squat whisky glass with the other hand.

It was true that John could be unreliable; he'd had a lot on his plate, after all. He'd challenge any man to walk a mile or so in his shoes. And now, while he was certainly being strict with himself, he entertained other thoughts that he knew very well already. John let these thoughts come in like old friends, shadows gliding through the windows: rain that was just starting to fall; and he got up to pour himself another, very small whisky.

The ball bounced faster and John began grimacing a little bit. It was *true*; Elaine was a Queen Bitch for stopping Benny from coming out to meet him whenever he wanted to. It would be much easier for John to get the later bus, and then the later train – cheaper too, most probably – but messing with John was Elaine's specialty, wasn't it? Elaine and her fancy semi in Plum Regis; John was paying for that semi with all the money he was sending, and now Elaine was living there with that prat Paolo, wasn't she? She'd moved on pretty fast, hadn't she? John didn't like the idea that he was paying for Paolo the prat to share a bed with his wife, but Elaine wasn't his wife any more, was she? John tried to count the years since he and Elaine had been together, living as a family with little Benny, in Paradise Block. It might have been eight years, John realised, shocking himself.

John's throwing hand was seizing, like a claw, and he shook it out before he started throwing the ball again; he threw the ball *gently*. John didn't want Elaine to be his wife, oh no. He wouldn't take her back, even if she'd been secretly spending his money on massive bulging tit implants. John chuckled to himself. The blue ball bounced up against the wall and back into John's hand. With Elaine it was all about control, she always had wanted to control John, and this was just another way of getting him right under her horrible thumb.

Truly, John thought that it was remarkable that he didn't feel annoyed. Instead, he felt heroic; John was going to see his boy. Even though Elaine wanted to keep him far, far away, he was going to see his Benny, his boy. The combination of the special whisky, the bouncing ball and the thought of seeing his son made John's eyes wet and he chuckled to himself again. This really was a special time in his life. John's worries were falling away of their own accord, the shadows were somewhere at the very back of his mind.

Now, John poked his head into the front room to see the camp bed that he had made up for Benny, carefully pulling the sheet taut under the frame and squaring the pillow, then mussing it a bit so it didn't look too perfect. Benny was going to be staying with his dad, not his fussy old mum, always trying to control everything. John nodded at the bed approvingly and then poured himself another little nip of whisky, but he kept saying the bus time and the train times over and over, steadying himself, completely in control.

John wasn't about to miss the bus.

It was 12.47 for the bus to the train station (that would cost him £2.50 just by itself, but never mind). The bus would get him to the station in time to catch the 13.39 train, switching trains to get the 14.02 from Upper Skein, with nine minutes to find the correct platform without having to talk to one of those stuck-up station assistants, or losing his ticket to Plum Regis, which would've cost him £22 already. John was so excited and the ball was a good distraction, but while John was repeating the numbers and bouncing the ball, drinking a little bit of this special-occasion whisky, he was thinking about whether Elaine had thought to buy Benny a train ticket back to Clutter (probably not), and if she hadn't, how much would a child ticket cost? And what age did you have to be to travel with a child ticket? John tried to count again, very quickly – how many years had it been since he had seen Benny? How old was Benny now? Of course John knew the answer to this, he knew how old his boy was, but other questions and ideas confused him: what would he do with Benny on the way back? It was a long journey and Benny was bound to get fidgety, that was natural, he was just a boy, just like John had been once, wasn't that right?

John's eyes were on the ball and he was thinking, *If I bounce this ball any closer to the bin, I'm going to knock it over, and I'll have to get down and clean it up, and then I'm likely to miss the bus, and the train, and the connecting train, and I won't be able to bring Benny back here, or give him this lovely blue ball that I bought especially for him.*

But John didn't want to knock over the bin because he had been *longing* to see Benny. And there was proof, if he ever needed it – John'd been telling his friends down at The Brass Cross for weeks: 'My Benny's visiting soon. His mother's finally given in, after how many years …' Then, 'The boy's coming up on Tuesday.' And finally, just yesterday, 'Benny'll be here tomorrow, so don't expect to see me in for a coupla evenings.'

But now that it was *the day*, John felt strange about a few things, silly things really; his furniture; stupid, nonsense things: his television chair – where would Benny sit when they wanted to watch telly? And would Benny even like to watch the same telly programmes as John? He'd been living with his mother and Paolo the prat; what if he'd changed, become pretentious? John wondered: would Benny want to eat different foods? Would he want healthy food; would he want vegetables? Maybe he would be vegetarian, like Elaine and Paolo the prat, or vegan; what was it that vegans actually ate, anyway? And what would Benny think of John's smoking? Would Benny have an opinion on *that*? Elaine certainly hadn't liked his smoking all those years ago, always trying to control him, but no, the ball bounced against the window ledge unexpectedly and came back at a strange angle. John spilt a little bit of his whisky but he managed to catch the ball. Benny was a chip off the old block, John thought, steadying himself. It wasn't fair to associate Benny with his mother, he hadn't been anything like his mother the last time John had seen him. John tried to remember.

It was raining outside and John saw the drops hitting the windowpane. Each life is like a raindrop, John thought. He saw that some raindrops collided and ran down the pane in one stream together, all the way to the bottom of the ledge, and some did not. John's thoughts were getting deeper, the way they always did when he'd had some whisky, especially whisky as good as this special-occasion whisky, and he thought, steadying himself again: *Some people just can't flow the same way*. John was nodding, realising that he was thinking some very true thoughts, and that he should probably have a little *more* whisky to encourage his brain, because that's just the way that John's brain worked.

People are different, John thought, they have different ways and habits and, sometimes, it's best to just leave them be. John let the ball hit the windowpane and disturb some of the drops, and then he started letting the ball go closer to the wastepaper bin, underneath the window ledge. He was thinking again, about Benny and his ways, and whether the boy might want help with his homework, which, John had to admit, he couldn't be bothered with. What did they learn in schools these days anyway? Pretentious things, most probably: poems and emotions. John had never needed those pretentious things.

Now John was thinking, *If I get too close to that bin I really am going to knock it over, and then I'm going to have to clean it up, and I'll miss the bus and the train and the connecting train, and I won't be able to bring Benny back here to my flat*, but then he remembered Elaine trying to control him. This is like an ultimate game of skill, he decided, and he started saying the numbers again to focus himself, 12.47, 13.39, 14.02, but with the whisky, and the excitement of the ball, and all these different deep thoughts, he was starting to forget what the numbers meant.

Thwack-thwack-thwack went the ball. John was concentrating so hard that he was sweating; he mustn't let the ball hit the wastepaper bin! Jesus, he'd be so annoyed if he hit that bin! But then, a sound from outside or *something*, an alarm might have started going off somewhere inside the building, and it startled John, and the ball *did* hit the bin and knocked it sideways, so that the bin spewed out hundreds of cigarette butts and tissues and old scraps of paper with things written on them sometimes. John stood up and slapped his thigh.

'God fuckin' dammit,' John said, looking around himself in disbelief. 'I'll have to clean it up,' John explained to nobody.

John went to get the vacuum cleaner from the cupboard under the stairs. He was mumbling, 'Got to get this cleaned up before the boy comes.'

John was down on his hands and knees. He used the nozzle to get up all the ash, and then he picked up the butts and tissues individually because they would clog the vacuum cleaner, and John couldn't afford to get a new one, what with all the money he had to pay Elaine. It was interesting, wasn't it, that John had to pay child money but Elaine still expected him to pay for Benny's train ticket and food and activities for the weekend when the boy would be at John's flat. Shouldn't Elaine pay *him* child money for those days?

John remembered Bill laughing with him in The Brass Cross: 'That's not how it works, mate.' They were goofing around, John and Bill. 'They want it all these days, these gals. They'll take the child money an' then call themselves independent women, an' on the same day they're dialling your number to bother you for more money cos the little-un's got it into 'is head that he wants a new pair of trainers ...'

John shook his head, crouched over the spillage from his bin. He had to deal with the little bits of paper, some of which John started to think he should never have thrown away in the first place. There were slips for jobs that John couldn't remember. He had no idea whether he had completed these jobs or not. John collected the slips and fanned them out on his table in the other room, resisting looking at the clock, even though the numbers – 12.47, 13.39, 14.02 – were singing in his head. John knew that he had to deal with the matter at hand, which he started to think might be quite urgent. The requests dated back to the beginning of the year, and although he'd ticked most as complete, he didn't even remember the majority. Had he been sleepwalking when he'd replaced the bathroom mirror in 17 and cleared the pipes in 21's kitchen sink? Had he really okayed the ceiling in the dark basement flat, flat 1, before the strange Fox couple had moved out? John saw that he'd scrawled, 'Large cracks around edge of room + bad smell in 2nd b/room – something stuffed in toilet?' on the slip next to F1; the whole ceiling was coming down! That would've been several weeks of work! He couldn't have ...

John grabbed a handful of slips, ignoring the telephone, a nagging little bleating ring-ring, and flinging open his kitchen cupboard, where he kept his plan of the block. John made sure to keep the plan up to date, with names of the tenants pencilled under their flat numbers, and little crosses when someone died, and F1, that was right, that was in the basement, where the crazy Fox couple lived, and surely he would remember fixing up the ceiling for the crazy Fox couple, the couple who had hoarded kittens and whose eyes were often seen spying from their little window at the foot of the building? John looked past the clock and up at his own ceiling, there were cracks there, too – Jesus Christ! The whole building might be falling down! What would Benny think? And, more to the point, were his tenants' lives in danger? John had given everything to Paradise Block, he had worked and worked to keep the building pristine and the tenants happy, it was an endless task, but it was John's task and he'd be damned if ...

John was steadying himself against the counter; something had stopped him feeling okay. He was getting old and there was so much work to do. Holy fuckin' hell, when would he get some peace? He just wanted to see his boy, to see little Benny ...

John glanced gingerly at the clock.

'Twelve thirty-five!' John gasped.

Would he be able to make it down to the bus stop in twelve minutes? There was a walk from Paradise Block to the bus stop, at least twelve minutes. Maybe, John prayed, maybe that clock was wrong. John hadn't changed the clock's batteries for a long time. John ran into the bedroom and grabbed his jacket. He pulled his mobile from his pocket – 12.36. The numbers leered at him from the greasy screen.

'Fuck!' John shouted, performing something for the blank walls, the picture of a young Benny on his bedside table.

John was feeling ill, all the little slips of paper were still on the table and as he ran around the flat, collecting up his possessions, knocking back a little more of the whisky, slinging his jacket across his shoulders and jamming his sockless feet into his trainers, John saw that there were cracks all over his walls and that the tiles in his kitchen were loose, they needed re-grouting. John sighed and sat down; he was wretched. Why couldn't he just have this one weekend with his son? How many years had it been? He felt the building consuming him. John had always put work first; he'd had to with the amount Elaine was asking him for in weekly cash injections, it was ridiculous!

From his window, John watched the bus plummeting over the horizon, as though it was held on elastic strings that never meant it to stop. It bounced along and out of view. He tried not to think about Benny and his disappointment. Benny was bound to be disappointed, but John knew that he could count on his son to understand. And John could send the ball first class; it would get there the very next day, never mind the cost of the postage. John thought about all the fun he'd had that very morning, bouncing the ball against the wall. It was a great ball; there was no question.

But when John sat down with another drink, he could see all the things that he had arranged, and how, when he had been arranging them, he was thinking of what Benny would guess about his father when he saw them. Videotapes were being sold off very cheaply, because nobody wanted them any more, so there was the old action film that Bill had watched with his son, *Die Hard*, which John'd picked out especially. There was the football trophy that he had won when he was just a boy, and that he had got out from the back of the cupboard, ready to show Benny. John remembered his own father, and wanting to show him this very same trophy. He could see himself holding the trophy, looking at the light that was held inside the circle, and tracing his finger round and round. What an amazing memory this was! And so clear! John felt like he could almost walk into this memory. He decided to pour himself a little more whisky, and snuggle down to think about that time some more, when he was just a little boy, just exactly like Benny.

But then, while he was pouring the whisky, some darkness started to come into the memory, and John looked at the water that had pooled around the bottom of his window frame and was mixed with black mould, the black eyes were eating the glistening raindrops. John was glad when the telephone started ringing again and he thought, *Bloody hell, it'll probably be one of the tenants complaining that I haven't been up to fix their something-or-other.*

John tutted. 'No rest for the wicked,' he murmured, taking the phone over to the table where all the slips still were.

'John Dodd, maintenance and upkeep,' John said professionally.

'Oh my God,' said the voice.

John saw the room swell, like the start of a migraine.

'Elaine,' said John. He thought about slamming the phone down straight away, running into the next room to hide, but he dropped into the chair by the table instead; it was like air whistling out of a balloon. John opened his mouth, he could explain himself easily, it wasn't exactly his fault that there were so many jobs mounting up, and she wanted her money, didn't she? And the bus, it was bad timing, that was all, and why did he have to explain himself to *her* anyway?

'You've missed the bus,' said Elaine.

'Stating the obvious is still your favourite hobby, then,' said John, preparing his righteous speech shakily, looking around for his whisky glass and darting into the other room to grab it, steadying himself with another swig.

'I had no idea, Elaine, but there were hundreds of jobs left off the rota. Some sort of admin error. The system is fucked. So I've gone and missed 'em, and now there's gonna be trouble. I mean, I'm keeping the whole building running, as you know—'

'Stop,' Elaine cut him off. There was some kind of shouting in the background, happy music. 'I don't want to hear it,' she said. Elaine changed her tone: 'Yes, aw, thanks for coming over, love. Don't forget your cake.' And then, 'Ben! Get Jake some cake to take home.'

John could hear Elaine moving away from the music, she started whispering angrily into the receiver. 'This is the last time,' she hissed, 'you're not letting him down again. And on his birthday!'

'Well, I've got him a present,' said John. He could give as good as Elaine, any day of the week.

'Oh, oh, oh!' said Elaine. 'Well done! Got him a present, did ya? Did ya hear that, Ben! Ben! Come here.'

John tensed. 'Elaine, Elaine,' he yelped frantically, 'you want your money ...' John tried to start an argument that they both recognised, one that didn't include him explaining this great big mess to his son, but Elaine was only half on the line.

'Ben,' she was saying, 'there's a special someone wanting to talk to you. Here you are, son.'

And then Benny was there, his voice a lot deeper than John remembered, more sullen-like straight away.

'Hellow,' he said (was that a bit of a posh accent John could hear?). 'Hellow, is it Grandma?'

96

John wanted to hang up the phone, but instead he said, 'You all right, son?' as casually as he could. 'It's your dad.'

And Benny said, 'Oh. All right?' maybe a little bit rudely, but what was to be expected, living with his mother, as he did?

'Listen,' said John, and he put on a funny voice, ''appy birthday! I would sing but, you know, I wouldn't wish that on my worst enemy!' Ha-ha-ha, John laughed, but Benny stayed silent. John swallowed.

'You still meeting me at the station?' said Benny.

He was being quite aggressive, John thought, but then again, John had always been straight to the point too – people had accused him of being aggressive, yeah, Benny was a chip off the old block, he'd be fine. John could still just hear the music jangling on behind Benny's voice, it sounded like Benny was having a great party, and John was glad.

'Well, son,' he said slowly, steadying himself, 'as it happens, I just had a huge number of jobs come in, and I missed the sodding bus, and your mother still won't let you out after dark, the soft old bird,' he added. 'So I can't make it this time, and I tell ya, I'm so disappointed. I've been chatting you up to my mates down at the pub all week. I've been saying, "Ah, my boy Benny's coming up any day now." But it's sod's law, the very day you're s'posed to be coming up, and all these jobs coming in, and your mother being so uptight, as she is, God bless 'er. I tried to tell 'er that you're old enough to be walking down the road five bloody minutes.'

John stopped to see if Benny wanted to say anything but he was silent.

'So you see—' he began.

'How old am I, then, John?' Benny interrupted. 'How old am I today?'

Benny didn't give his father much time to reply, and the numbers appeared again, dashed around in John's head – 12.47, 13.39, 14.02 – confusing John and making it impossible for him to answer in time before Benny mumbled, 'Twelve. I'm twelve today, John. And people don't call me Benny any more.'

'Is that so?' John said. He tapped his knuckles twice on the table and then scratched his chin. John had always called his son Benny. 'Why's that, then?' he asked, but the line had gone dead, and Benny was gone.

John held the phone for a few seconds and then dropped it back into its cradle. Of course Benny was a little bit disappointed, but John had promised himself that he'd send the ball first class, and he would, early tomorrow morning, any twelve-year-old boy would love a blue ball like the one John had bought for Benny. John glanced at the requests on the table; he was less paranoid than he had been before. He could make a start on these after he'd sent the ball, the very next day. John brushed the requests into a big pile and put a coaster on top, so that they didn't disappear somehow.

But while he put his jacket and his cap on again, John started to feel more upset about Benny and not seeing him on his birthday, for some reason, because he knew that Benny was fine and that he'd definitely go and get him next year, there were going to be plenty more birthdays, and John would go and get him right from his front door if he had to. Benny was probably busy hanging out with his mates, causing trouble, and that was where he'd rather be anyway. John looked out at the rain, which had started falling steadily again. Sometimes it's better to just let people be, he thought, it's not good to always be forcing people into spots they aren't happy in – let them be happy where they are. He tugged his curtains closed.

John was wheezy on the stairs, the bloody lift was broken down again – another thing he'd have to see to – and he kept hearing a sound right behind him; there were several footsteps, all at once, and the wind kept cracking on the windowpanes and through cuts in the glass. The staircases in Paradise Block all looked the same, nicotine-coloured wallpaper with the odd rip, scatterings of damp black fingermarks around the light switches, but as John was clambering down, he felt sure that he'd passed the same floor several times: wasn't that tear in the same spot? Hadn't he seen that notice, 'KITTENS FOR SALE, call 07*********' on the floor above? John's flat was five floors up, right at the top, five sets of stairs and he should be at the main entrance, but John counted six and then seven, and the footsteps continued right behind him, *thwack, thwack, thwack*, and stopped only briefly when he turned and shouted, 'Fuck,' and then, *thwack, thwack, thwack*, again, just as though Benny's blue ball had got out of the flat and was following him, bouncing from step to step, pounding after him, until finally: John saw that the corridor was getting lighter.

Outside, John was panting and he stopped for a moment to watch a balloon floating over the top of The Brass Cross and the shrivelled little building that used to be the Grisco shop, then further off, towards the town centre, the department store, and the railway station where trains left for Plum Regis every two hours. It must've been a funeral balloon, or something, because it was dark, not brightly coloured the way balloons usually are. John didn't like to remember but he did anyway, because that was just the way that memories were and, in his head, he could see Benny, almost down to the yellow salt that had always been crumbing around the corners of his eyes and the thin line of grime snaking around the inside collar of his football shirt, the freckles that covered his cheeks and nose, a handful of gravelly sand.

John was very drunk now and he'd forgotten that when he became this drunk, by himself, as he was, he couldn't stop the memories coming in. And so, it was Benny and John at the fair, where everything was ridiculously over-priced and the fair people had rigged all the games so that you lost your money trying to win some piece of tat you never wanted anyway. Benny was crying about wanting to go on some stupid ride that cost an arm and a leg and only lasted a couple of minutes, and John had been trying to shush him because Julie Perkins-White was there, and she kept looking over.

In John's memory, Julie was just a blur of yellow hair. Julie always had her hair done, permed and yellow, and she had nice clothes, a cracking figure, didn't she? John tried to concentrate on thinking about Julie, but trudging across the gravel towards The Brass Cross, his head down, little flecks of rain needling at him, he kept seeing Benny and remembering how embarrassing his screaming had been, how he had started howling, as though someone he badly loved had died. What kind of boy would scream over a ride? John hadn't known what to do so he'd just talked to Julie over the top of Benny's screams. He would've said something like, 'Kids, eh? Always wanting something,' but John remembered that Julie's kid, little Tamsin, was staring at Benny, all wide-eyed. John had tried to pinch Benny while he was still talking to Julie, to try to shock him out of it, to stop him embarrassing himself, but that just made Benny wrench away, and then Julie was able to tell what he'd done because Benny said, 'Ow!' and he started rubbing his arm over and over, so dramatically, like a little grass.

And even though John could tell that Benny was putting it all on, Julie had started to back away, saying something pleasant, probably; Julie was a nice girl, with a cracking figure. John remembered the fair person, muddy teeth and purplish eyes; he had been behind Julie, and John had gone, 'I know what'll cheer my Benny boy up.' And the fair person came over, straight away, his mad eyes sparkling at the thought of a sale; his horrible little smile.

Tamsin had picked a pink balloon. 'Thank you very much, John,' she would've said, while John paid the extortionate amount that the fair person tucked into his pocket, but Benny just stood, staring up at the bulk of balloons, snot still dripping from his nose.

John had said, 'Which one then, Benny?'

John looked back at Julie, smiling, and then back at Benny, starting to look stern again, most probably.

'Blue's your favourite colour,' he told Benny, 'why don't you have a blue one?'

Then John could see that tears were starting up again in Benny's eyes and Julie was saying, 'Thank you ever so, John. We're going to get some candyfloss now. Say goodbye to John and Benny, Tamsin,' and John heard her voice moving further away already and then, looking down at Benny's pale little face, something inside him had snapped, and he started shaking his son.

'What balloon do you want? What balloon, you little wuss?'

And Benny was screaming again now, and Julie was saying, 'Oh, oh, oh,' and then Benny started trying to say something, coming out so slowly, with John still shaking him, and 'B-b-b-b-ut,' said Benny. Julie came and kneeled down next to John, probably thinking about what a bad deal this poor kind John had been cut, having such a sulky sissy for a son. The boy was almost keeling over with tears, he kept bending, like someone had punched him in the stomach, and people were looking, and Julie said, to calm him down, 'You don't have to get a balloon. That's okay, Benny.'

Benny looked at Julie and he said, all of a sudden calm, which just showed how much he'd been faking it, 'The balloon will get away. I don't want to have it cos it will get away, and then I'll be sad.'

John had laughed, cuffing Benny on the shoulder; as if they were sharing a joke, and just so glad that he had finished crying. He would've said to Julie, 'Kids, eh?' or something like that, but Julie, yes, John remembered now, she was into some sort of magic crystals and spirituality and had come around to see Elaine with little oils in brown bottles, she held Benny's head against her hip as if he had said something very clever.

Julie said, 'Benny's afraid of being abandoned by his

balloon.' Then Julie held her hand to her heart and made a face that was saying 'aw'.

Surrounded by rain and concrete, John watched the dark balloon floating away until it could no longer be seen and thought, for just a second, about how *they* had floated off, only a few weeks after that day at the fair. John had let Elaine and Benny float into their new life, their other life without him. He was no longer responsible for Benny, he had his child – fifty-odd flats, each with dripping taps and cracked foundations, paint jobs to cover scars and expensive window replacements to heal the broken eyes of the building. John was bewildered and he stood, halfway between The Brass Cross and Paradise Block, almost hearing Benny's voice: *The balloon will get away*, and then, the rain started to get stronger and drops were sliding down the bridge of John's nose and pinging from the peak of his hat.

The barmaid greeted John with a big smile. This was his favourite barmaid, the one with the lovely red hair, Stacy, her name was. And seeing Stacy's face seemed to affirm what he'd been thinking all day, that he should end up in The Brass Cross, where he belonged, where people understood him. John decided that he'd get Stacy a drink in, too, even though he remembered one other time when she'd poured herself a double vodka cranberry and cost him £4.75, but that was okay, because Stacy kept an eye out for him and served him first when the bar was busy, so really it was like saving time, paying for the odd vodka here and there, and it especially paid off on days like this when the rain or something else, perhaps the fact that twelve-year-old Benny had been sniffy with him, had got him feeling very upset, actually, and a big smile from a pretty girl was really exactly what he needed.

John chuckled to himself; he was starting to feel better already.

Bill Standing and Les Harwood were already sitting at the bar, they came out of their conversation and looked as happy to see him as anyone could, chorusing, "Ello John!' both at once, and John smiled. John had given Bill a bit of work, and Les was a good lad, wasn't he? John felt fondness and friendship, camaraderie, he might say, and he chuckled at his own pretension, at the warm feeling that was growing.

'You all right, John?' said Bill, and he cuffed him on the shoulder.

'The usual?' Stacy said, and John beamed, feeling delighted and completely at home.

'And one for yourself, love,' he said jubilantly.

Les and Bill waited while John arranged himself at the bar. John clasped his fingers around his first drink and took a long gulp, feeling almost tearful after the day he'd had.

'Your boy not coming down today?' Les asked, and John shook his head darkly, still gulping down the delicious bubbles, feeling some escaping down his chin but knowing that he wouldn't be judged for it. Bill and Les would never judge him; they were good, decent friends.

John breathed out, he was shaking his head. 'The bitch wouldn't let him,' said John, and he put his drink down. Les and Bill stared at John, disbelief in their eyes. Stacy brought her drink over and leant on the bar in front of John, ready for John's story. John could see the top slices of the barmaid's breasts and he savoured the moment, taking another huge pull on his drink; he was like a soldier, getting ready to go to war.

'I missed the sodding bus,' said John. 'Sod's bloody law.'

Bill and Les nodded sagely. 'They never come when they're s'posed to, do they?' said Bill. He was the more assertive of the two men; some people said that he was trouble, but John felt like he was one of the best guys he had ever met. Bill was like a soldier, too.

'That's right, Bill, mate! They never bloody do, do they? No offence, Les, mate,' said John, remembering that Les's old man had been a bus driver.

'Nah, you're all right, John, mate,' said Les. 'They never bloody do!'

And the three men were laughing together, Stacy going, 'Yeah, yeah, you're not wrong.'

John carried on, 'So if I wasn't catching the bus then I wasn't gonna be catching the train, and the bitch was all like this ...' John put on a high voice that didn't sound much like Elaine's but had Les and Bill sniggering. 'I'm not letting him out after dark,' John simpered, and he carried on in his own voice, still very loudly to show his outrage, 'Train station's only five minutes down the bleedin' road!'

Bill and Les stopped laughing and they started shaking their heads darkly again. 'It ain't right,' said Les, and Bill offered to buy him a drink.

'You were really looking forward to your boy coming down,' he told John, and he put £5 on the bar. 'Get John a drink, Shell.'

John smiled gratefully at Bill, who was affirming the

rough deal that he'd been cut, but he felt a little odd that he'd forgotten the barmaid's name, the one with the lovely red hair. She was his favourite barmaid, wasn't she? John glanced at Shell's chest again and saw the picture of the baby that Shell kept there, the disc containing its potatoey face. That's right, Shell had a baby; she was always talking about that baby. Thinking about the baby unsettled John now, as though Shell's life outside the safety of the pub was spoiling things somehow. John let himself drink the whisky quicker than he usually would have, feeling the finger beckoning to him and allowing it to pull him in towards the dizzy softness that was waiting.

"'Ere,' said Les, 'I'll tell you what my ex-missis wanted when we split up,' and John replied, excited, 'What *didn't* she want!' and ordered another round of drinks, preparing for Les's story, which he chuckled at for the first part and then listened with a half-ear, staring at Shell's miniskirt and the little drink bottles behind her legs; brown bottles of honey wine, tomato juice, pineapple crush, orange fizz; some of the bottles had a picture of a smiling woman on their fronts. Beneath the drinks there was an empty shelf with cobwebs and black marks where bottles had once sat; the shelf seemed to go back for a long way because it was so dark and dirty, and John didn't want to look at it for long. It seemed like that spot was the only inhospitable place in the whole pub; why look there?

So John focused his tired eyes back on the glistening bottles, listening to the tones of Les's story, and then he was thinking, what was Benny's favourite drink? John wondered vaguely, did Benny like women, smiling women? Did he like girls yet? What would Benny think of Stacy or Shell, or whatever her name was? Did Stacy or Shell know *his* name? Did John matter to Bill or Les, or Benny, or Elaine, or to the tenants of Paradise Block, who never thanked him for the jobs he did, just went off to tend to their babies, or washing, or whatever was boiling over on the hob? And as he drank more, John struggled to listen to Les's story about his car and something else that was about the fish in the pond in front of his house, and he was thinking about the blue ball, and the music that he had heard playing at Benny's birthday party, and the numbers that he had repeated to himself that morning began to haunt him and John Dodd thought, over and over, 12.47, 13.39, 14.02, listening to the pounding of the rain that was attacking the windows behind where the men sat.

Complaint

The department boss is waiting at the bus stop with ordinary shoppers and staffers and the girl doesn't have time to hide or look down at her phone.

'Oh, hi!' the girl says, and the department boss replies, 'Didn't see you there,' puts his arm around her head. He is a lot taller than she is but this is supposed to be a hug.

The girl has known the department boss since she was younger, a teenager, since she first started looking for employment at the department store. He has talked about throwing her bits of extra work, hours here and there. Last year, there was a Christmas party where the department boss called the girl 'Sexy Bum' and grabbed at her, underneath the bottom of her coral-coloured skirt that matched her coral-coloured top; but nobody had noticed. The girl wasn't even a proper staffer, so she had just stood very still until the hand stopped, flopped back into the department boss's lap. She hadn't been worried enough to make a complaint at the time and she isn't worried about it now, particularly since she is wearing her drab uniform: tonal shades of cream and silver, matching the walls of the department store, even saggy stockings that match the tiled floors rather than the colour of her own skin, even clip-on earrings that bear the emblem of the store, and a maroon headband that matches the gum of the escalator handrail; and anyway, the department boss is barely looking at her.

The bus comes, so they get on to it together, the department boss and the girl.

'I'm moving to the other department store soon,' the department boss tells her, 'Plum Regis.'

They are standing up and shoppers and their children surround them, some staffers, all leaning over or around the girl, reaching up to hold on to poles so that they don't fall over. The department boss is more comfortable, nearly standing next to the driver, holding on to his own pole.

'Oh, cool,' the girl says, trying to remember the Plum Regis store. In her head, it looks identical to her own building, a vast white whale-fish with silvery window scales, but the girl's mother often talks about the Plum Regis store; says that it is superior, that it has a better range of departments.

'What department will you be on?' the girl asks.

'Well, my dad died,' the department boss says, ignoring the girl's question. 'My mother says she's lonely.'

The department boss shrugs. The girl is thinking about her hours, the bits of work the department boss has talked about chucking her. She wonders whether he is going to an inferior department at the Plum Regis store, something like Foot Odour, or Builders' Cement. Could she go and work for the department boss in Plum Regis, on Foot Odour?

'Oh no,' the girl says, 'that's so sad.'

'Well, I might not go,' the department boss says, and the girl realises that he thinks she is sad that he is leaving, not that she feels sorry for his lonely mother. The girl looks at her hand, clinging to the pole. She relaxes her grip and breathes through her mouth.

'I should probably stay,' he says, like he is thinking out loud. 'My departments will deteriorate without me.'

'You're right,' the girl replies, 'you're a great department boss.'

Some shoppers get off the bus and the girl and the department boss go upstairs to sit down. They look out of the window. There is a bloody sunset and three shoppers are trying to take photos of it as the bus creaks past some clapboard houses. In one front room, a woman is hanging a strand of tinsel on an economy department-store tree; the tree is slender, with only four branches, and it stands like a man, the tinsel draped ridiculously around its neck. The girl's stomach rumbles and she remembers that there is no food in the cupboard at home, one packet of White Fingers, only one biscuit left, and this is the communal packet, so the girl's flatmate might have already found it. She looks around; there are several children on the bus, sitting next to shoppers, or even by themselves, but they all seem to be immersed in games on their phones, or in staring at their hands or knees. The quiet stillness on the bus is making the girl feel like she might say something absurd, something odd or strange. 'Flighty' is a word that the girl's mother sometimes uses to describe her.

But it is the department boss who fills the silence very suddenly: 'You've sent me your CV, haven't you?'

The girl nods her head sheepishly.

The department boss has asked for her CV several times in the past and she has sent it; her personal information and the department that she works in, Glassware. The girl's information only takes up a very small portion of a page. Now, the department boss takes out a small notebook and adds her name to a list. The girl is surprised to see her name there, so firmly written, so fixed and normal. Some of the other names have question marks beside them, some have been underlined or crossed through, but for now, the girl's name is untarnished, inscribed in the department boss's book.

'Thanks,' the girl says, and the department boss finally returns her smile.

'You scratch my back,' he says, and before she can reply, he starts talking about someone he doesn't like at the department store: Dorian Bell.

Dorian is fairly new and has long hair, which he wears tucked behind his ears and slicked with gel. It is part of the uniform to have your hair controlled and neat, but you can see that Dorian's hair is almost abnormally lustrous when a strand escapes. Dorian works on Glasses – eyeglasses, not Glassware – and his department is very popular. The girl has heard that Bookmarks and Leather Chairs want to be moved because Dorian's section is always chaotic, spilling over with shoppers, especially women shoppers. And these women shoppers are often nearly blind, so they knock books over; and they are rude, or in love, so they are always flopping down in the chairs, even the ornamental chairs, which are not for sitting in; and they are forever trying to open the ornamental books, which cannot really be opened but are just for the displaying of bookmarks.

'Dorian doesn't understand the fundamentals,' the department boss is saying. 'It isn't necessarily about selling; it's about shopper well-being. The shopper should have whatever they want, whenever they want it, even if they *don't* want it. If Dorian sells all of his frames to shopper A, B and C on a Monday, what will happen when shopper D visits the department store on Tuesday, and is sent away disappointed?'

The department boss talks like he is reading out of a big, grand book, and he doesn't seem to mind whether the girl answers him or not.

'What Dorian doesn't see is that eventually, even if he doesn't make the sale on that particular day, the shopper will come back, and they will have changed their mind; whatever it is, the shopper will have had time to think about it properly, and that toaster, or hosiery, or set of golf clubs, will finally be revealed as very appealing ...'

While the girl listens, she remembers Dorian Bell in the food court. Dorian had asked her whether he could chuck her a couple of hours on Glasses. He said she had a good face for glasses, a good, plain face, *moonish*; she could model some of the frames. Dorian said he liked the girl's moon-face; he liked her *lunar* energy. He wanted to expand Glasses, to take over part of the third floor. This had never been done before; usually, department bosses just took on other departments and then went to senior management, but Dorian had a *vision* for Glasses. The girl remembers that he had a tangerine and he kept peeling the pith fussily, laying the white strands next to his plate; he had a tall glass full of fragrant tea and he ate small potatoes by throwing them into his mouth.

'I know,' the girl says bravely, 'he told me that he wants to open his own store.'

The department boss closes his little notebook, puts it in his pocket.

'His own store!' he says.

'One right here, or maybe even in Plum Regis,' the girl replies, pointing in the direction of Plum Regis, beyond the crumble-down houses. She smiles shyly, pleased that the department boss is laughing.

'Fat chance of that crackpot ever owning anything,' the department boss says, over-amplifying his laughter. 'My God, do you know what he said to our receptionist the other day? He stood right in front of her and said, "Don't you think that's a *magical* tree outside?"'

The girl raises her eyebrows.

'My God,' she mimics, 'a magical tree?' The department boss is still bellowing laughter and she says, spontaneously, 'Dorian Bell is far too strange to be a department boss.' The girl is carried by the laughter, giddy, and even though the bus is very quiet, she yelps, 'I don't know what those women see in him – his hair is *ridiculous*, for a start.'

The bus stops and they watch some shoppers getting off, disappearing into little streets, pulled into houses by invisible threads. A taxi turns the wrong way into traffic and the air is full of horns.

'Well,' the department boss is quieter, he grumbles, 'I've got nothing against him because of his *hair*, per se. You know, we're not just a bunch of stiffs up in management.'

The sunset is orange; it bleeds and strobes through the aisle of the bus. The girl stares desperately into the brightness; she shouldn't have mentioned Dorian's hair, and now she knows that she must not look at the department boss; she must not see his pale blond hair, his widow's peak, his waferish scalp.

'No, no,' the girl says, 'I didn't mean that you were stiff, a bunch of stiffs I mean. Department bosses are sensible – *clever*,' she finishes feebly. 'And what is Dorian talking about ... a *magical* tree?'

She laughs again, but she has lost the department boss, he retreats into himself, as though Dorian Bell is with them on the bus, throwing his lustrous hair around. The girl tries to remember whether she has ever seen a tree anywhere close to the department store, let alone a magical tree. The land adjacent to the department store is barren because of the footfall and traffic surrounding it; there is nothing except the car park and the bus stops, two lanes of traffic, one to deliver shoppers and one to take them away. The department boss is writing something in his little notebook, shielding the page childishly, so that the girl can't see.

'I'll tell you something,' the girl says; the sound of the pencil on the paper is making her itch inside, it grates on her. While she takes her phone out of her pocket, she feels like her arms are moving slowly, like she too is animated by a set of strings.

'What?' the department boss says; he is sulky, petulantly pretending offence, he puts on a woollen hat and then takes it off again, huffing. The girl wants to give him a treat; she feels, momentarily, like she is holding a ball of fire, it blisters between her palms.

'It's a text from Dorian,' the girl tells him. 'He says it's a poem.' She giggles.

'What?' The department boss snatches the phone. He starts reading lines aloud, incredulous, as if he can't believe what is written there.

'He asked me for my CV ... He was going to chuck me some hours.' The girl clears her throat, not wanting to show any similarities between the department boss and Dorian. 'But he just took my number and sent me this poem!'

The department boss ignores her, flabbergasted. 'What a prick!' he says.

'Don't tell anyone,' the girl says. The bus is nearly empty now and she feels the stillness again, wants to ask the department boss to lower his voice. Dorian had once given the girl a pair of empty frames with a twisted arm, and she'd pulled the arm straight and worn them to a department interview, and— The department boss is laughing and she laughs with him.

'It *is* pretty strange,' she says, trying to grab at her phone, and then giving up, sitting with her hands in her lap. It is cold and she plucks at the fabric of her skirt, bandaging her fingers. 'At least we know he doesn't just fancy trees!' she laughs.

The department boss stares at the girl for a few moments, before his loudest peal of laughter bursts into the quiet air. 'At least he doesn't just fancy trees!' he repeats, and then he goes dark and hisses, 'That freak.'

'Oh God,' the girl says and then, 'It's just silly, really. Don't tell anyone,' she repeats.

The girl doesn't want Dorian to find out that she has shared the poem, even though she's sure he's sent similar messages to lots of girls at the store. The girl isn't even outstandingly pretty, just moonish. *Flighty maybe*, she hears her mother's voice, but no, not that pretty.

'I won't, I won't,' the department boss says. He's zipping up his jacket, still smiling. The girl notices some snot stains on his cuffs. She glances out of the window and thinks: *Is the department boss going to get off here? Is he going to one of these houses?*

'Forward it to me, though, would you?' he asks her, standing up out of his seat, looming over her now. 'I could do with a laugh.'

The girl is giggling again.

'Send it for my Christmas present,' he jokes.

'I will,' the girl says, and then, 'Not really, though.'

It is only just December, but the girl imagines thinking about the department boss on Christmas morning, when she is with her mother, and wonders if she will, accidentally.

'What was it?' he says, moving away from the girl, down the aisle of the bus, 'When I'm in your magic orbit ...' He's clearly trying to commit the poem to memory: 'your sparkling face ...' The department boss looks so happy. 'My God,' he says.

The girl watches the department boss walking up a street that leads to a cluster of nicer houses, perched on top of the debris of the surrounding neighbourhood, icing on a cake.

She thinks that if he turns around he might wave.

The girl is still warm from the laughter, traipsing up the long black stairs inside Paradise Block. She realises that she has shared a moment with the department boss, and she rereads the message from Dorian, shaking her head and laughing to herself. 'My God,' she whispers privately.

When the girl gets inside, she sees her flatmate. The flatmate doesn't have any hours; she spends most of her time inventing reasons to hang around the department store, spying on other staffers and insulting them: *That one on Stockings looks like she's about to drop dead*. The flatmate has a little moustache, grey and timid-looking, not bristly and black; still, though, she cannot afford to buy facial bleach, and that's not the only problem. When the flatmate moved in, she had come with a bottle of sour, toad-green wine, and she had told the girl about her childhood, how once she had tried to escape, to climb out of a window, and – *pow!* – the frame had crashed down. Now her fingers are bent, this way and that, and, although she sometimes wears little gloves, can sometimes hide her moustache under a layer of foundation, the flatmate has always found it very difficult to get hours. Of course, this isn't why the girl doesn't like to spend time with the flatmate, not at all; it's more that recently the flatmate has become depressing and snarky, *desperate*; but today, the girl feels shaken or excited by the conversation with the department boss, and she lingers in the kitchen.

'It was funny on the bus,' the girl says, 'I bumped into that department boss.'

'Sexy Bum?' the flatmate asks.

'Sexy Bum, yeah,' says the girl, 'but we had a laugh together.'

The flatmate stops stirring her tea, rests her strange hand alongside the cup. The water is pale grey and the girl can see that the bag has been used several times already.

'You had a laugh?' the flatmate asks the girl.

'Yeah.' The girl looks in the cupboard. 'I showed him that poem,' she says casually, 'you know? He thought it was hilarious.'

The flatmate is looking at the girl and her black eyes probe her.

'Humph,' she says, 'you'd better make sure he doesn't get the wrong idea.'

The girl has found the communal biscuits. White Fingers. There is only one left and the girl has shown the flatmate, forgetting what she was doing, forgetting to hide and save the biscuit for herself.

'Last one,' the girl says to the flatmate, confessing. The flatmate takes the packet.

'Bet he'll be after you now,' says the flatmate, putting the biscuit into her mouth, 'if you had a laugh with him.'

Crumbs fall over the flatmate's lip and on to the floor; she uses her foot to scurry them away, into the crease between the cooker and the fridge.

The girl gets into bed because it is very cold in the flat; she isn't thinking about the department boss or Dorian Bell. Her stomach sounds like a storm. On the bedside table is the pair of twisted eyeglasses and some broken pieces that her supervisor asked her to throw away: an elephant with one ear, a candlestick that she keeps upright with a mound of plasticine, one glass saucer that she has carefully glued back together and is now covered with shiny pennies that she has saved.

When her phone buzzes the girl is lazy about finding it in the grey bedclothes. The girl's mother usually texts her at about this time, asking when she's going to get some proper hours, some stability. *You can't continue flitting around, department to department.* The girl's mother worked on Scarves and then in the office at the department store for many years, until her eyesight began to deteriorate, but she says that she can't afford to keep subsidising the girl, making up for her failures: something's got to give.

When the girl finally unearths the phone, she sees that the message is from the department boss. Her naked feet are sticking out of the end of the blanket and she pulls them inside, close to her body. The girl doesn't have many clothes, her nicest pieces are hanging on a thin brown rail at the edge of her room, and she can see the coral-coloured skirt and the matching coral-coloured top. *Is that skirt too short? Is the top too tight? Were the bright colours aggravating to the department boss?*

'It's probably about work,' she murmurs, reasoning with herself.

Either that or he's after you.

I was going to mention it earlier, but Min Dimorier is having severe problems with her legs. Thought you'd want to know.

The girl reads the words several times. She hardly knows Min Dimorier; when she tries to recall her face she comes up with something between a hen and a woman, long dresses and beige jowls, a pecking head. Min is old and works in a department miles away from Glassware, on the lower-ground floor, what is it – Stockings? Why does the department boss think that she wants to know about her legs?

The girl writes, Oh shit, and then deletes it. Oh no, she writes. The girl's thumb hovers; is Stockings one of the department boss's departments?

Oh no, that's awful. Send her my love.

Love? Should she say, 'regards'?
Hope she's okay, she adds.

The girl feels like she is being dragged into something; is the department boss trying to imply that she could take Min's hours? If Min can't stand any more: if Min *falls down*?

The girl tiptoes across the room and goes to hover outside the flatmate's door. They have rented out the front room to a third girl who has a boyfriend and is never at home, so there is no living area, only bedrooms and the narrow galley kitchen. The girl is about to knock when she hears her phone buzz again.

The girl scuttles back to her own room.

Still laughing about that message. I might have to write you a poem too.

Immediately after this message, there is a message from the girl's mother and the buzz makes her jump.

I've got some warm scarves here for you. From Scarves.
Any luck with hrs.?

Not yet, the girl writes to her mother, and: thank u for scarves.

She sits down on the corner of her bed; the laughter has faded out of her body, like water disappearing down a plughole.

Ha-ha, she writes, so funny! (:

For another week, the girl is jumpy when she receives a text; a mixture of excitement and foreboding; she waits for the department boss to say *Hey Sexy Bum*, to offer her something that comes with consequences, but soon the girl has almost forgotten about the department boss and the texts. The store is so large that she regularly doesn't see anyone she knows for days and days, so she goes about her business, her menial jobs. Hardly anyone wants to buy the glassware, the ornamental paperweights with bursts of green and red oil inside, the candleholders that are so heavy and have such stern corners. This is nearly Christmas time and every week the girl can count the pieces she has sold on one hand.

The girl doesn't expect to hear from the department boss, but when she does, she is stoic about it. She thinks that maybe she can coerce him into chucking her some work this time, after the laugh they had shared. And the department boss is actually asking her when she is next working at the department store – he wants to know what hours she has.

But then—

Could you pop up to my office and say hello?

The girl holds her knees together on the bus. She feels self-conscious again – she has never been to the department boss's office, any department boss's office.

When she gets home the flatmate is holding a bowl of cornflakes, her crooked fingers are linked across the china; she holds the bowl with both hands. The flatmate has obviously been doing laundry because there are beige legs hanging from the rack near the ceiling and the windows are misty. The girl comes up behind her.

'Hi,' she says.

They stand together, amongst the hosiery legs.

'What's happened?' the flatmate says. She puts a spoonful of cornflakes into her mouth but then she throws the whole bowl and spoon into the sink and spits.

'My milk's a bit off,' she says, almost apologetic. 'Thought I could get away with it.'

She puts her mouth under the tap and drinks.

'The sink will smell if you don't scrape it out,' the girl says.

The girl and the flatmate look at the water and milk, the cornflakes floating around.

'The department boss texted me,' the girl says.

'Oh God,' says the flatmate, smiling and then frowning, looking at the girl's phone.

'He wants you to pop in?'

'Yeah,' the girl says grimly, 'what do you think it means?'

'You can't say no,' the flatmate says, 'he's your boss.' The flatmate says the girl's name.

'He's a department boss,' the girl agrees, as though she is stunned by the thought.

They are both silent.

'Pop in,' the flatmate repeats, 'say hello.'

'Have I done something bad?' the girl says.

'Or worse,' the flatmate says, 'he's after you, Sexy Bum.'

The flatmate giggles briefly; like they are girlfriends, but she looks quite nasty, her little moustache drawn back, her very dark eyes mirthless, and the girl wishes that she hadn't told her.

'You might lose your hours,' the flatmate says.

The girl looks at the flatmate's curdled milk in the sink again and goes to her room.

I'll pop in on my tea break, but I've got a bad cold, so won't be able to stay for long!

The girl spends the morning staring at pieces of glass, unable to concentrate on the mundane jobs she usually commits to: looking for fingerprints and attacking them with her J-cloth, repositioning price stickers, ordering money into the correct sections in the till, and so the time passes very slowly.

The supervisor has been visiting another department and has come back with a crate of surplus air fresheners. She is a very haughty supervisor, even though she is old and has grey hair, and the girl can see a bogey in her left nostril, eyecrumbs at the corner of her eye.

'Look,' the supervisor says, 'pine fresh. Room Odours let me have them. They've been printed incorrectly, but they smell lovely.'

The girl smiles weakly and looks into the box. The fresheners are shaped like trees and have ENIP HSERF written across them.

At 1.20 p.m. the girl goes into the bathroom, takes off her headband, and reapplies hair serum. She doesn't want to look too good, but more, she wants to look normal; she doesn't want to look strange. *But how would the department boss make her look strange?* Maybe he has written me a poem, she thinks, maybe he wants to read it to me. On her fingernails, the girl is wearing nail varnish that coordinates with the mosaic on the cubicle wall; one fingernail blue, one cream, one purple: this is part of the uniform for female staffers. The girl touches the wall and matches her nails to their correct tiles; with her hand outspread, the fingers look like they could press through the wall and the girl could step inside, become part of the department store. The girl takes her hand away. She applies more serum without looking; trying to imagine what she would do if the department boss performed a poem, what parts she would tell him she liked, where she might smile bashfully, how she might get out of the room. Then the girl sees that she has applied too much serum and that her head looks wet, oily.

'Shit,' the girl whispers. She tries to wipe the serum away with some toilet tissue but it just separates in her hands and bits get stuck in her hair and look like dandruff.

The office is very far away. While she walks the girl thinks about how it often feels like the department store could almost continue to run without the people, without the shoppers, the staffers, the department bosses, even the senior management. She listens to her shoes in the empty corridors, looks at the steady yellow light and the clocks that are patterned around the whitish walls, ticking onwards. The girl tries to spot shoppers or staffers in the long beige expanse; she has the vague idea that she might see the flatmate who often walks past Glassware and pretends that she's surprised to see the girl, as though she might be shopping for a new decanter or a sparkling figurine. Five departments have passed before the girl sees any sign of life, and then it is just the flick of an apron tie as a staffer disappears behind a display of White Fingers on Biscuits.

The girl doesn't use the customer lifts, but she does run up each of the maroon-gummed escalators that are cutting slothfully through the centre of the department store, whirring placidly. Still, she only has seven minutes of her tea break left when she gets to where the department bosses live, at the very top of the store.

It is an office full of many people, working and talking on big white telephones, some watching their staffers on specially installed CCTV, others looking at pictures of stock or napping with blankets that match the branding of the girl's uniform. The department boss is in one corner, and the girl notices that he doesn't have his own cubicle walls, although he has a list of his departments printed boldly and glued to the side of his computer – the girl sees Min Dimorier's department, Stockings.

The department boss is talking to someone, the telephone cradled between his shoulder and cheek, and when he sees the girl, he holds his hand up to say, *Stop, don't come any closer*. The girl tilts backwards and forwards on her shoes, rubbing her hands together as if she is cold. She only has five minutes of her tea break left and she wonders what her supervisor will do to her if she is late.

A woman with a watery grey face is sitting near to the girl and she tries to see what she is doing, whether she might be making lists of the departments and their bosses, or if she is doing an inventory on the number of sale stickers that are used by each department, both jobs that the girl's mother enjoyed during her time at the store.

'I work on Glassware,' the girl says, but the woman just smiles, moving her lips like it is a huge effort, like she is lifting an enormous crate using only the thin line of slippery mauve lipstick.

When the department boss is finally finished on the telephone, he gets up and walks towards the girl, not catching her eye.

'Right then,' he says, 'this way.'

He guides her around to another set of doors that require a code. The girl remembers the elephant figurine on her bedside table, the candlestick. The receptionist is inside the corridor, talking to a department boss who laughs at what she says, but when the department boss and the girl pass, they are silently staring at them.

'I've only got a few minutes,' the girl says, 'my supervisor will be a—'

'I know,' says the department boss, holding the door, 'you've got a little cold, right?'

The girl remembers her lie. 'Yes,' she says, and she sniffs a bit.

Inside the room is another man. He has her record up on a computer, her CV and her passport scan.

'Hello there,' he says, smiling. *Very nice teeth*, the girl thinks, *maybe he manages Toothpaste*.

'Hi,' says the girl. She looks around to see if the

department boss has left and sees him sitting at the side of the room. The other man is obviously waiting for her to sit down. She sits and sees a plastic triangle on his desk: STORE MANAGER.

'Now,' says the store manager, 'don't look so worried. You've done nothing wrong.'

He hands her a tissue.

The girl remembers waiting until 5.30 to stamp her timecard after she'd already shut the department, playing on her phone in the back.

'It has come to our attention,' says the store manager, looking deeply into the girl's face, 'that you have become friendly with the Glasses department. Dorian Bell, isn't it?' He is using one hand to scroll through the girl's information while he looks at her, still smiling, many of his teeth showing. The girl sees CCTV footage of herself standing by the till; she moves joltingly towards a podium and lifts up a glass shoe, puts it back down and twitches back to her original position.

'Oh,' the girl says. She looks at the department boss, but only momentarily; she doesn't want to make him feel accused.

'We're all humans, we all have human needs,' the store manager tells her, 'some more than others,' he adds, laughing in the direction of the department boss, 'and we all like a staffer who can let herself go ...'

The girl becomes pink; her coral-coloured top and coral-coloured skirt, dancing with the Room Odours girls, skidding on the dance floor: *flighty*.

The store manager recrosses his legs and steeples his fingers.

'You know,' he says, 'you can give your phone number out to whomever you like; it's just—'

'I didn't give Dorian my number,' the girl says.

'Sorry,' the store manager says, furrowing his brow, looking at her even more keenly, 'something's not making sense to me.'

The girl waits for the department boss to tell the store manager the truth, but he is silent.

'Dorian wanted me to do some hours on Glasses,' she says quietly, her voice barely a whisper. She doesn't want to make Dorian Bèll out to be like the department boss, although they had both wanted to chuck her some hours, they had both taken her phone number from her CV.

The department boss clears his throat in the corner as if this is his cue. 'It's just completely out of line,' he says, talking to the store manager.

The girl looks from one man to the other and realises that the store manager already knew that Dorian had taken her number from her CV, he already knew about the poem; she wonders why he didn't just say so.

'But I only showed you as a kind of joke,' the girl starts.

'It's natural to be upset,' the store manager tells her, 'this is, after all, sexual harassment.'

The store manager says 'sexual harassment' like the words are something delicious on his tongue.

The girl glances at the clock and sees that she is due back from her tea break.

She stands up.

'It's the end of my tea break,' she says, as if this would mean that she could go.

'I'll write you a note,' the store manager tells her. 'You

can tell your supervisor that there's been some kind of trouble.'

The girl sees that the store manager has been making a list of employees and that Dorian Bell's name is at the very top. Min Dimorier's name is also there, written in pencil.

'Trouble?' the girl asks.

'What's your supervisor's name?' the store manager wants to know, writing 'Dear', at the top of a page in slippery writing.

'Trouble?' the girl repeats.

'Well,' the store manager replies, 'you're very upset, and the store could receive a hefty fine if this isn't dealt with correctly. Sexual harassment is really bad news.'

'We don't want you to feel like you can't take any extra hours,' the department boss says. 'We were just talking about Min Dimorier and her leg problems ...'

The girl holds her knees together. CCTV footage continues on the computer, but the girl sees that she is doing everything right: now, she is taking the money out of the till, carefully smoothing the notes under a stapler. The girl begins to feel a little more relaxed.

'I thought it was strange,' she begins, but the store manager and the department boss start having a private conversation.

'This is what you get for hiring remotely,' says the store manager. 'If I'd got eyes on that hippie crackpot before he started, I'd never have let him through the door.'

The girl remembers the Sexy Bum party. Dorian Bell dancing all night, right under the disco ball. A few supervisors flitted around the edges of the floor and the rest of the room was a swirl of colourful dresses. Dorian's gel had been overcome by sweat and his hair was loose on his shoulders; there were small heels on his shoes and they thumped against the dance floor like a heartbeat.

'He's a freak,' the department boss says, 'a tree-hugging freak.'

'And he wants his own store!' the girl says, dropping one of her little Glassware gloves in her excitement. 'In Plum Regis,' she quotes, reaching down to pick up the glove awkwardly.

'And so many sick days,' the department boss replies, ignoring the girl's comment about Dorian's store, 'magic trees obviously not doing their job.'

'He fancies trees!' the girl nearly screams.

The department boss and the store manager are still laughing with the girl, but then they begin shaking their heads.

'My God,' they say.

The store manager types angrily until Dorian Bell's file comes up. There is no picture on his CV, which is a shame because Dorian is very handsome, and this is one of the reasons why his department is so popular; there is just line after line of experience and credentials. The girl feels light and breathless, as if she is witnessing something miraculous, but then she understands properly what is happening, and the air in the room thickens.

'You're going to fire him,' the girl asks, 'because of the text?'

'We just can't tolerate it,' the store manager says, listening for someone to pick up the phone.

'But I didn't mind,' the girl whines, 'we thought it was so funny.'

'Well,' the store manager says, his hand over the receiver, 'it's not really a joke if the store gets a massive fine, is it? Do you think sexual harassment is a joke?'

The department boss stands up, and looks at the girl; her mouth is still open, so she shuts it. The store manager is saying hello to someone now, and the department boss types in the code, opens the door to release her from the office. The girl looks at the pad underneath the store manager's hand. 'Dear' is smudged across the page, and for a moment, she considers trying to tear the page off so that she has something to present to her supervisor.

'Come on,' the department boss says, 'we've got things to do. Can't be rescuing damsels in distress all day.'

The girl is already ten minutes late back from her tea break.

'Could you write me a note, please?' the girl is saying, but the department boss is marching off towards the grey-faced woman, and when she catches him up, he puts up his hand again. The girl waits, clutching her gloves and watching the giant clock in the middle of the office, and then, when the second hand has gone around three times, she runs towards the door and all the way through the other departments, Oven Supplies, Parasols, Coffins, Gym Shoes, down in one of the customer lifts, past Body Lotion, Silverware, Sunscreen, Skin Conditions, the long beige corridor that snakes through the departments is stretching on in front of her and her shoes clatter endlessly. The girl is panting like an animal by the time she arrives at Glassware.

The girl sees that the flatmate is there.

'Hi,' she says.

The flatmate is glassy-eyed.

'Oh, hi,' she replies.

The girl notices that the flatmate is wearing a uniform; the department store's logo is displayed across her left breast. The flatmate wears little gloves, and she has put something on her moustache, it looks sticky, and the girl recognises the scent of her hair serum.

'We thought you weren't coming back,' the flatmate says, her lip glistening.

'Who did?' the girl asks, looking around for the supervisor.

'She said you'd quit,' the flatmate tells her, acting like she is startled by everything. 'She gave me this uniform.'

The girl stares at the flatmate who is arranging money in the till, her wonky fingers surprisingly efficient with the different-coloured notes and coins.

'I just came in to do some shopping,' the flatmate explains, reaching into her new apron and pulling out a tissue. 'Here,' she says plainly. 'I didn't have *any* hours,' the flatmate tells the girl.

Now, the supervisor is squeaking along the division between Paper Cups and the girl's Glassware section.

'Oh!' she says, mock dramatic. 'How kind of you to grace us with your presence.'

'I was with the store manager,' the girl says, holding on to a podium for support. A tiny figurine of a girl dances across a frozen pond with a tiny boy. 'Please,' she begs, 'I need the hours.'

The flatmate has moved on to the coins now and she is noisily sifting through the 2p trough to make sure there are no silver or gold coins there.

'She needs the hours!' the supervisor scoffs. 'I can't just have girls waltzing back from their tea breaks at God knows when,' she says. 'We've been rushed off our feet down here.'

The girl looks around, there is one customer at the very limit of what she can see; it is a man holding up a giant box of ant powder in Pests. He is trying to read the back of the packet.

'I just ...' the girl says. 'Please.'

She feels faint and remembers that she hasn't eaten that day; she tries to visualise what foods there are in her cupboard: an egg, a rind of black bread and one, maybe two, packets of broccoli-flavoured pasta. The girl feels the Glassware section tilt, like a chessboard being lifted up and shaken; she says her flatmate's name as she falls: 'Pinkie,' she calls to her, but the flatmate isn't there when the supervisor picks her up, handing her an envelope with wages for the hours she has worked that day inside.

The girl looks at her flatmate, who is searching for fingerprints on a glass duck.

There are twelve exits to the department store and the girl goes out through the seventh, down through the car park at the back where some old women are begging, sitting inside cardboard boxes, like little boats floating alongside the mighty ship of the store. They reach up their arms as she passes by.

The girl walks all the way around the department store, which takes fully fifteen minutes. She is cold and tired, but she wants to check: there is no tree, magical or otherwise.

On the bus, the girl's phone buzzes. It is the department boss.

I couldn't let Dorian act that way. Especially not with someone I care about.

The bus rumbles beneath the girl and she feels the emptiness in her stomach.

Thanks for looking out for me, she writes.

She puts her head between her knees while she waits for a reply, and when she sits up properly again, she sees that the old man sitting opposite is staring at her. The girl doesn't want to look at him properly because he is clearly disapproving, and she spots the pin that department bosses wear on their lapels, but this pin is purple coloured, not the usual green.

Always a pleasure, the department boss has written.

Any chance of some hours on one of your departments?
My supervisor hasn't got anything for me in Glassware.

She adds a kiss at the end: X.

We'll see, the department boss replies.

There is another sunset; only this time it is yellow and purple. From her seat upstairs, the girl sees Min Dimorier, walking with a stick. The girl starts to cry and across the way, the old man with the purple pin shakes his head. He is holding his hands very stiffly in his lap and his back is straight.

There is another text before the girl gets off the bus:

How about I treat you to dinner in the food court on Friday?

And then:

Sexy Bum.

The girl is walking, dragging her feet. Her shoes haven't even been paid off yet; she still owes Work Shoes three payments, and now she feels like every step inside them is a heavy burden. The girl stops to blow her nose and notices that the old man has come off the bus with her. *Maybe he's going to kill me*, she thinks dramatically, excitedly. She imagines the flatmate finding her body later, a mannequin in the Paradise Block car park. The man acts like he is going to brush right past her on the narrow street, but then he stops, alongside her.

'I'm not in the habit of giving out favours,' he says, looking the girl up and down excessively. 'My God,' he mutters, 'you young girls.' He shakes his head. 'You look like you really need to get yourself together.'

He opens his jacket and takes out a silver holster, snaps it open and removes a card, waving it in front of her like he wants to whisk it away. The girl follows the card with her eyes until he stops, holds the card still so she can take it.

'Thank you,' the girl says, from between her tears, 'thank you so much.'

It is a business card with the man's name and email on it and the address of the other department store, in Plum Regis. This department boss works on Rubber Gloves. He has a similar hairstyle as the Sexy Bum department boss; the girl notices that he has flakes of skin on the shoulder of his smart department boss jacket.

'Now,' the new department boss says, 'send me a copy of your CV. We'll see what we can do about chucking you some hours.'

Doctor Sharpe

'I'll see you soon,' I said.

A heartbeat.

'Let's hope not,' said Dr Omar Sharpe.

He smiled, even though my throat had closed up, and my eyes were filling with tears.

'What I mean to say is, we don't want any more accidents, do we? We don't want you hurting yourself, Rose.'

That was the first time he ever said my name and I marked it in my diary as a turning point.

I wrote: 'Today Dr Omar Sharpe said my name. This marks a direct change in my life.'

I would have written more, but the box for 22 July was too small, so I just drew a small black heart in the top right corner, and then I drew another one in the left corner. One is mine and one is his.

Dr Omar Sharpe has pictures of naked women on his computer. I know this because I went into the clinic the other day and we talked.

He said, 'What are your symptoms this time, Rose?'

This was the second time that he had ever said my name, but I didn't mark it in my diary because of what happened next.

I said, 'Well, I have been getting dizzy and hot and I have some marks on my thigh area. They are like faint welts.'

Dr Omar Sharpe said, 'Okay, could you get on to the bed for me, please?'

He said this quite tersely because he was worried about being tempted by my body again.

'Are you feeling dizzy right now?' he asked me.

He came closer and I said, 'Oh yes, Doctor, I feel dizzy and hot, so hot.'

He looked at me and I let my mouth open slightly. I was wearing gorgeous pink lipstick; the shade is called Fuchsia Fun.

'Could you show me the welts, please?'

I struggled with my jeans and did actually start to feel quite hot.

'Sometimes they disappear, though,' I said. 'Sometimes they are here and other times, they are not.'

I was wearing my very best panties, they are virgin-white lace with a bow, but he didn't look at them. He just looked at my thighs. The doctor was transfixed by my thighs. He handled the flesh like it was dough, like he was baking a cake with my body, transforming it into something delicious to eat. I smiled to myself because, I have to admit, I was *surprised* that he found my thighs so enticing. My body is inconvenient because I have stripy scars and a few large blemishes: some moles that have faces inside them, and hairs that twist away from my skin and stand there, bristling chattily. I have always felt that there was a secret message, somewhere on my skin – this message made people act strangely towards me, sometimes imagining that they couldn't see me at all – the message was blaring out, flashing atop my shoulder or just behind my knee, places where I couldn't cover it over properly.

But Dr Omar Sharpe was different, the message didn't come through to him, or else he ignored it. He was fascinated, transfixed. He smoothed my thighs and massaged them; he pinched my flesh between his fingers.

Finally, he said, 'It doesn't look like there are any welts here.'

'Why don't we wait a little bit longer, Doctor?' I said. 'They tend to come back every five to ten minutes.'

'Could you bear with me for a moment?' he said.

While he was gone, I felt his office come alive around me: his brown swivel chair; his stethoscope on the desk, tiny flecks of pale yellow ear wax on the rubber buds; his pens and pencils, some of the ends chewed; the blue head of a biro gnawed into a point. And then I looked at his computer and the mouse and the keyboard, all of which were grubby from the times that Dr Omar Sharpe had rubbed them and touched them with his fingers. My heartbeat quickened when I realised that somewhere inside the computer there was a file that was labelled Rose Durrell and that in that file were details about me, that he had written, there might even be details about love, possibly.

I got up off of the bed and pulled up my jeans. I didn't

do up the button in case he came back in and I had to quickly pull them down again and jump back on to the bed.

I am quite used to using the computer because I have been a member of several new dating sites and had to write my profile information (I said that I was interested in shopping, sewing and rescuing endangered animals, when really my interests are television, eating and sex). But anyway, this was to my advantage now because I managed to flick through his files quickly.

Dr Omar Sharpe had a very complicated system. I tried to think like him, to unpick the difficult names of the little yellow folders, 'Spinal – Plum Regis 060693'. I didn't panic, I felt the warmth of his hands on my thighs, his breath on my ear and amongst it all I found one, 'girls' it said. Of course I clicked; after all, I *am* a girl. But inside the folder there were just miniature women in thumbnail, their legs spread open and their heads back, eyes closed: ecstasy. I scrolled through the small women quickly, using my left hand to stop my right from shaking too much to hold the mouse. The women were mostly brunettes with fair skin; I bit my lip as the realisation hit me: they were broad-shouldered with large breasts, they wore white underwear, they all looked like ... They looked like *me*. There were footsteps outside the room. I leapt backwards and the chair skittered across the floor like an octopus.

'Oh good,' said Dr Omar Sharpe, 'you're dressed.'

I understood that this was a sensitive moment for him, and so I just said, 'Yes.'

'Well, surgery is closing in five minutes.' He looked at me, scribbled quickly on his prescription pad and handed me the note. 'But please do come back if the welts reappear.'

'Oh, I will,' I said.

Driving home, I stopped at a set of lights on the invisible line between Upper Skein and Plum Regis. It had begun to rain and I looked at a fly that was caught and drowning where the bonnet met the windscreen. I watched the fly's legs cycling through the air until cars began beeping and pierced my thoughts. I realised that Dr Omar Sharpe had been locked in a psychological prison, fantasising about me constantly. The thought made me feel awful and I stopped at a garage at the edge of Clutter, to buy crisps and a sleeve of scarlet jam tarts.

But then, when I got home, the living room didn't feel so lonely, warped through with dream light; my collection of china animals seemed more lively, their usually impassive eyes glinting at me sassily; the kitchen suddenly had character; the greying roses that were shrinking into themselves in the hallway, they looked romantic, like forbidden love.

I was desperate to see the doctor, but I satisfied myself that evening by tipping the prescription note back and forth between my hands, and over parts of my body. The note was slick, almost fluid, like oil. I thought about the women in the 'girls' folder, how contorted their writhing had been, as though they were shedding their own skins, like sexy snakes. I looked at the words that Dr Omar Sharpe had written, the same note he gave me every time, and they changed shape in the darkness of the dream light, everything was unpeeling in front of my eyes.

For sleeping: Zopiclone, 7.5 mg, Rose Durrell, Flat 17, Paradise Block, Box Close, Clutter.

I began to see new words that he had meant to add, strange anagrams appeared in the dream light; and the neighbours, who were shouting at each other on the other side of the wall, only inches away, their words started to melt on to the page. 'How can you, Rose?', 'You're just sleeping', 'You never take me to Paradise', and just when I was starting to drift away, the doctor's hands all over my body, I noticed some secret marks at the edges of the paper's skin, inkless scratches.

In the kitchen, under the humming light, I took a small pencil and scrubbed over the edges of the paper, spreading the eelish shine across the front, as well as the back, so that the paper was like a grey fillet of fish. Now I could see the prints, borne hard into the actual flesh of the paper, the letters that said, 'rose, rose, Rose, ROSE, Rose, rose', over and over, as many as would fit.

I was surprised when I called the Plum Regis surgery the next day.

The receptionist answered. There was nothing unusual about that.

'Hello,' she said. She has blonde hair and she wears it in two plaits. The receptionist acts like a little girl but also wears short skirts and boots up to the knee. I know why that is.

'Hello,' I said tersely.

'Oh, it's Ms Durrell, isn't it? Oh ...'

The receptionist covered the receiver with her hand to

make everything muffled, but I could hear her twittering to someone else who was obviously there. I wondered who it was, whether perhaps Dr Omar Sharpe had asked her to forward my calls directly to his office.

'Ms Durrell? Are you there?'

'Yes,' I said. 'I'm not going anywhere. My legs are covered in enormous welts.'

'Oh,' she said.

She cleared her throat, as though it was full of sharp blades.

'I have been asked to tell you, Ms Durrell, I have been asked to tell you that Dr Sharpe can't see you any more. He would like to advise you that you may need to see a *different kind of doctor*.'

She covered the receiver again. I imagined her neat red nails digging into my legs, my arms, tearing at the flesh.

'Hello,' she said.

'Hello,' I said.

'You shouldn't come here any more. We know you don't have welts on your legs. This is just a small surgery. We've got lots of people to see. You need to see a different kind of doctor, one that can help you, you know, mentally.'

She paused.

'Hello?' she said.

'Hello,' I said.

'Dr Sharpe has sent out a letter, Ms Durrell. I have to go now.'

One of the soaps was on the television and a woman was there, ripping up serviettes and smashing bottles in the pub that they all go to, shouting wildly about her true love who had left her, so I watched that for a while, but then when it finished there was nothing left for me to do but sob in the shower while water ran out of my eyes and all over my body.

The next few days were very difficult, but I quickly realised that I had to find an excuse to get into the Plum Regis surgery, to see Omar. I needed to make myself sick, and fast. I wondered if it was possible to infect yourself with life-threatening diseases and found lots of places on the internet that said you could and gave lists of foods and drinks and products that would do just that. So I did an online shop for almost all of the things on the list (apart from green olives and dark chocolate because these are foods that I absolutely hate and will only resort to after all other options have closed to me).

I also ordered five packets of cigarettes.

When the order arrived the young delivery boy looked very concerned. He was red in the face.

'Don't worry,' I said, 'I'm *trying* to get cancer.'

He walked away quite slowly.

I consumed everything within the first few days: brown bottles of sugar drink and fried doughnuts covered in watery white glaze, plates and plates of dark red meats and curls of ham, some fish, too; the majority of the foods were the bodies of animals, thin sausages of blood pudding, speckled with fat inside like a cut thigh. One fish was still complete behind the film that covered the packet, and I saw a scar that ran along its cheek and over where its eye had been. I was interested to see this history of pain in the life of the fish, and I looked for other signs, but there were none, so then I cooked it and cut it and ate it. There were eggs with dappled shells that I boiled and peeled and, for the first time, I noticed how perfect they looked underneath, glowing brilliantly and smoothly on the plate, and I had to smush them, one after another, into my mouth. I smoked the cigarettes over the next week. It wasn't as easy as you might think for someone who has never smoked in her whole life. But then, sitting still and waiting, looking at the needles of egg shell and all of the empty packages littering the table, I realised that it would probably take a long time to give myself cancer, probably longer than Dr Omar Sharpe would remain in love with me, probably longer than it would take for the dream light to fade.

I sat opposite the curtains on a stool, with one eye staring out of the crack between them. Outside, the concrete was apricot in the dusk, the shouting of little boys and girls, thwacks of footballs, an ice-cream van; clouds melted and white cats scuttled across the ground, cars sparkled in the distance. Nobody came and nobody went, the telephone did not ring.

Omar, I thought, *where are you?*

All day long I watched the television or stared out of the window, it was raining all the time, and the rain began to look just like the fuzz of static on the screen. I usually take care of myself but now I forgot to eat; maybe this was the revenge of the animals I had consumed, the flesh had piled up inside; I was not hungry at all. I didn't miss the food, and when my selection box of cakes went hard, and the icing began to crack like an old foot, I did not feel sad. I only felt lonely.

My best friend Elaine, who used to come and talk to me about lipsticks and what eyeshadows suited me the most, about how I could be a younger, *better* me; she hadn't called by for years now. I only ever made a single purchase: Elaine sold me the Fuchsia Fun lipstick for £4 incl. VAT, and it came with instructions and a small poem that didn't rhyme but was all about the power of womanhood. I cut the poem out and stuck it to my fridge.

Live in the dream light;
The power to change;
Peel away the layers;
You're living inside;
It's Fuchsia Fun.

Now I missed talking to Elaine about how I could transform myself and my body, and looking, in amazement, at the parrot earrings that dangled alongside her face.

It was later that week that I took my bath and the neighbours were playing very loud music and I thought again, *Omar. Omar Sharpe.* And then suddenly, as if from nowhere, I realised: Omar Sharpe, Sharpe, *sharp.* And I jumped out of the bath and nearly fell down the stairs, running to the kitchen to open up all the drawers, and line up the utensils like a little hopeful army of men on the worktop.

Outside, everyone in the world was the same, and the sky was dark for so many hours, but inside, there was dream light, and the blood was thick and heavy.

It was difficult to drive, that is all I am saying. I am not one to complain, I rarely grumble. But it was difficult to drive because I had made several incisions on my hands and this made holding the wheel very painful. Making the sharp turns left and right that the journey to Plum Regis required stretched the wounds open wide, like hungry laughing mouths. Also, my face was covered with wounds and blood kept running from my forehead over my eyebrows and around my eyes. And I could smell it, which is really horrible and bad, actually. It smelt like blood pudding in my little car. But I didn't care. Even when I was creating the incisions, looking underneath my skin, *unpeeling*, I didn't feel the cuts, not really. I just thought of Omar.

And when I arrived, when I pulled into the Plum Regis Surgery car park, I was delighted because there was a space next to his car, his dark blue, royal blue, his Audi.

At Reception the receptionist sat, as usual, stacking appointment cards, and when she saw me her mouth dropped open, but I just said, tersely, 'I would like to see the doctor, please.'

'You ...' she said.

The receptionist often looks right past me, but now she seemed lost for words, and I started to worry that she was angry about the red stain that I had left behind me but then I thought, *I can't help that! I'm critically ill.* And I said again, 'I want to see the doctor, please.'

'I think she'd better see the doctor. Look at her arms! And her face! Her cheek is coming away!' said an old woman who was sitting in the waiting room, holding a trembling copy of *Fantasy Gardens*.

'Thank you!' I said, and turned around to beam at the woman, but then I realised that my cheek really was coming away, and I took off my rain hat to hold it against my face. It wasn't that I was impatient, but every moment that I was not with the doctor was agony, and then also I was starting to feel actual agony because I had cut myself over fifty times.

'Ms Durrell, this is the last time you will see the doctor. Ms Durrell, what have you done?'

'Get me to the doctor,' I said simply.

The receptionist pressed a red button with a single red-tipped finger and she spoke, 'Dr Sharpe, we have an emergency out here. Could you come here, please? Dr Sharpe?'

But before she had even stopped talking the saloon doors of his surgery room opened and he was there, a silhouette against the bright synthetic light.

'Jesus Christ,' he said.

And I thought, *Yes, you are. You are Jesus Christ.*

'I'll get a wheelchair,' he said.

And he did and he put me down, not altogether gently because of the stress that he was under seeing me like this.

When we were alone together he gave me an injection and I slept. In Dr Omar Sharpe's office, there was a poster of an idyllic beach, with 'Aloha' written in the corner, seashells peppering the sand and a beautiful woman swimming, far away in the crystal-blue sea. The last thing I saw was his face, in front of this poster, and the last thing I heard was, 'Fucking hell,' but those curse words sounded so beautiful to me because, because they meant that Dr Omar Sharpe, they meant that he cared about me.

While I slept, I dreamt that we were together in the dream light, on the Aloha beach, but that I had left my body, that Dr Omar Sharpe and myself inhabited the bodies of dolphins, and our rubbery skins were identical and bumping up against each other, our squeaking gurgling sang over the sound of the waves.

'Rose, Rose, Rose, Rose,' I heard, in dolphin language. 'Rose, you're only sleeping.'

After I came around to consciousness, the doctor seemed even less calm and collected than he had been before. He had finished stitching my wounds, and I looked with wide eyes at my hands, which were filled with tiny little bits of pink string. My body was tied together, strapped back into place. I tried to think that Dr Omar Sharpe had decorated me, that he had made a *new, better* me, but as the tingling drugs started to fade away, I began to feel very much like myself, heavy in my skin.

'You've done an excellent job, Doctor,' I said.

'Ms Durrell,' said the doctor, 'I want you to listen very carefully. Look in the mirror.'

He held up an oval mirror, framing my face securely in white plastic.

'You have ruined yourself,' said Dr Omar Sharpe. 'You have destroyed your life, your opportunities. These scars will never heal.'

I tried to laugh, as though the doctor was joking, but the stitches in my lips and around my mouth strained horribly.

'Surely you must see me as more than my looks?' I asked him.

I remembered the secret message, flashing and shouting – maybe the doctor had understood it, after all; perhaps he had liked it.

The doctor cleared his throat impatiently and began writing on his computer. I tried to look, to see if he was writing what he really wanted to say, whether he might bring up a picture of one of his 'girls', but he turned to me sharply, and he looked as though he was going to speak, but then he changed his mind, and he called for the receptionist to take me away.

As I drove home to Clutter that evening I watched myself in the rear-view mirror. It was very dangerous but I barely looked at the road. I thought of my old face, the face that I had tried to escape; the face that a fine doctor had loved. *The face that Dr Omar Sharpe had dreamt about.* My stranger's mouth turned downwards and upwards at the same time. The split lip had been sewn but it was jagged. Dr Omar Sharpe had *not* done an excellent job.

There was a letter in the post. It was a viciously bright grey day; the cold light was shining through the windows. The letter had been sent first class and the address had been typed on the front, a standard label attached. Inside, there was a prescription note, the same tedious slip of paper that Dr Omar Sharpe usually sent me away with, thin and meaningless, with a dark, livery underside that was slick to the touch. I stared at it for a long time and then wandered into the living room, where the curtains were closed and the sofa was plump and damp-feeling, waiting for me to sink into its folds. The letters that were written there; Dr Sharpe's handwriting, the loops that strangled and imprisoned my name inside of themselves, trapped me like I was no more than a single word: *Rose*.

The note was signed with Dr Omar Sharpe's formal signature, just an ambiguous grey scribble, with one slipped tendril that looked as though it wished it could reach up to touch my name with its hands but couldn't, *it would not*.

The next day, I phoned my mother's machine for the first time in seven years. I was astounded that the phone hadn't been disabled; the payments must have been coming from an account somewhere, draining the rest of her money away very slowly.

'I met a man, Mother. I thought I had fallen in love. But it turned out, you know, it turned out that he was completely shallow. He only wanted me for my looks. He wanted my body. It's only lucky that I found out in time, Mother. You always told me—'

The answering machine cut my message off, but I listened to the sharp dialling tone for several seconds, looking at my broken face in the misty hallway mirror, smiling and grimacing, kissing the air with my jagged lips.

Black, Dark Hill

Underneath the boat, our girl's shadow is kicking her legs. Up there, inside the boat, her boy is reading – it's just a pamphlet that he has taken from the hotel, but her boy will not be disturbed. He is basking in the sun and he looks luxurious: definitely a god or an imp of some kind. Our girl has diligently taken coupons from the newspaper, put on her dress and the summer gloves to hide her strange fingers; she has shaved and primped and plucked; her boy has driven them in his car. They have come out to Lilybank River, our girl and her boy, it is their first holiday together, away from Clutter, away from our girl's responsibilities at home – her job, the rent, the cleaning, and the extra tasks she has to do to earn her place, searching with her dark eyes for little spaces she can live in.

Her boy has eaten all the black bread sandwiches, vinegary egg and sprigs of window-box cress; he has scoffed the boiled sweets that splinter like shards of glass, but our girl doesn't mind – she is amazed at how she can adapt, change her personality, her body, even the hungers that she has, all for her boy. Our girl sees boat after boat, all kinds of couples; they are taking photographs and grinning, sometimes wearing matching T-shirts and hats. A stand beside the Lilybank River is selling cigarettes, long red ice-lollies, and a large display of wilting liquorice, brown sticks impaling the stand. And there are giant sunglasses, the type that incognito celebrities wear; necklaces hanging from the roof, cheap golden medallions; these cast a false glint on the dark river: pirate treasure. Our girl thinks that she might want to buy a pair of sunglasses, or some cigarettes at least, but they have already drifted past the stand, and somehow, she knows that she won't be coming back along the Lilybank River, not today.

Our girl fidgets and glances nervously at the black water.

Our girl's shadow can see everything: the other shadows are holding on to their boats, hiding themselves in the smooth darkness. There is rubbish in the water, discarded necklaces and sunglasses, strands of slimy liquorice melting into the riverbed. Our girl's shadow sees a tangle of old fishing wire. She thinks about trying to moor her boat and clamber up inside, to join her two pieces and be with her boy: to slither all over him, whole; but she is worried about letting go for long enough to grab hold of the wire.

Our girl's shadow holds on to her boat.

Her boy is whistling; he is very relaxed, stretching out his bare feet, his yellow soles and the crabbed toes. His hair is mussed and sticks up in little points, the dimming light making fire inside his curls. Our girl's shadow can feel her real self, up inside the boat; she is shifting, trying to talk to her boy while she rows. The river ends at a waterfall where they are supposed to turn the boat around, come back the way they came. Our girl can already see the black, dark hill in the distance, where the water plummets downwards. It is only a small waterfall, a natural waterfall, so there is no mechanism, no shadow underneath. There is nothing that waits to pull them in, wanting to grind their thin bodies around and around for ever.

Our girl irons a crease in her dress with her gloved fist; some black grime has made a 'V' on the airy pink fabric. Her boy hadn't wanted to stop to release her dress, trapped in the car door, and she had worried about flinging it open while they were moving. He had sped through the little, veiny roads towards the Lilybank River, away from our girl's other life, where she drops coins, clattering into the till, cleans the same blank windows with a solution called *Pow!* Now her boy is sleepy, drowsy, having arrived at the river, secured our girl in the boat. 'Plenty of time for all *that* later,' he says, pointing at his watch, miming to our girl, like she is a child. Our girl looks at her boy's feet again and imagines gently splitting the slight webs between his toes with her tongue.

'Just relax,' her boy is saying, 'just try,' he tells her. He is looking at her, arms behind his head and fading golden sunshine falling all over him; he seems very loving. Soon, our girl might kiss her boy; wiggle her wetness into his red mouth. Our girl looks at the soft skin around her boy's armpits, and feels the absence of the black bread sandwiches. She used to eat a lot, enjoying all kinds of foods, but then she changed; our girl had been surprised that she could make such fundamental alterations, but now, even so, her arms ache and she is starting to feel very hungry.

'It's just the two of us,' her boy tells her, his goodness glowing. 'You don't have to be so needy.'

But our girl knows that there is part of herself underneath the boat, keeping the boat steady, hiding her face, her crooked, probing fingers. It feels unfair that, even though she is away from her responsibilities at home, the nagging demands of her life, she is still hiding what she wants, all of her hungers. Our girl keeps looking at her boy, basking in the sun, and then back at the murkiness of the dark, black hill and she drops the oars, letting the boat drift slowly along the river (and feeling something. She is feeling something strange, unusual: is this something bad?).

Our girl sometimes has very bad feelings.

Now, our girl sees that there is a little bit of water coming into the boat, at the far end. She starts to say something to her boy, but he tells her again, 'Just relax.' Her boy is shaking his head, smiling about something private, something only he knows. He tells her, 'You're just insecure, sweetie.'

Her boy trails his hand through the black water, he drops sweet wrappers and they look like pearls of rain. Underneath the boat, our girl's shadow can almost touch his fingers and she is transfixed, staring at the pink smudge on the water until the hand suddenly disappears, and she hears thumping overhead. Her boy is trying to stamp on some ants that are in the boat.

'We'll never get rid of them now,' he says, as the boat begins to wrestle, to spin and tremble under his feet. He accuses our girl: tells her that *she* has spilt the lemonade; the lemonade that has been prepared specially, funnelled into little brown bottles during our girl's busy days. Our girl's shadow feels our girl standing up in the boat, flapping her sweating hands. She feels the crash as our girl falls to her knees in front of her boy, sticky lemonade splashing her knees and thighs, clinging to the little blunted hairs. There were going to be biting kisses, slow-eyed rubbing and nibbling, *he had said that he was hungry*, but now, her boy is annoyed, looking at our girl sideways while she moans and pants on her knees. He leans back in the boat, draping his leaflet over his eyes, as if nothing is happening.

Our girl's shadow looks at the other shadows; they sway like reeds, a garden of outstretched arms. The other shadows look very tired, running around underneath their boats, taking care of things, ensuring that their boats stay safely on course, that they don't fall down, into the black, dark harshness, where there is a frightening tangling of legs and arms, and where they are destined to drift (and our girl's shadow realises that she is very tired, also).

Our girl's shadow has a plan.

The Lilybank River is becoming darker. Our girl sees a willow tree, branches splaying over the river, long fingers dangling in the water, and she steers the boat so that it stops amongst the branches. The fingers of the tree, the way our girl takes off her gloves to tickle her boy's skin and writhes on him; this all rouses her boy, and he lets her touch his cherry-stone nipples under his shirt until he sees her dark eyes probing him, her body grow excited, and he yelps, his voice trembling, 'Don't be so easy.'

Her boy still wants to punish our girl.

'Do you want the boat to capsize?' he hisses, and our girl sits back, her strange hands resting on the puffy hill of her skirt, considering. Our girl doesn't know whether she will sink in the water; will she float on the surface, a deceitful pattern of rosy light?

When our girl's shadow finds the right point, where our girl's knees and her boy's feet have weakened the wood, our girl's shadow gets her fingers inside the boat. She is surprised at how easily it comes apart. Our girl's boat begins to fill with water. Our girl feels the water soaking through her plimsoll, and then her sock; her toes are wet, wriggling; and she waits quietly, looking at the insects that scurry away from the dark pool, the reddening of the wood, the leaves that quickly float on the surface like golden suns.

Soon, her boy begins shouting at our girl, up inside the boat; he tries to grab, to reach out for the branches of the willow tree, but the tree may as well be made of paper, it is sharp but weak, it slices his hand and disintegrates into little pieces of brown; the dead branch is like charcoal, like smoke. Our girl's shadow works faster, pulling and pulling, until the boat collapses underneath their feet, and bits of wood spread across the Lilybank River.

*

The other shadows watch silently; their eyes are dull and cloudy and very still in the water, their greyish skin blends with the mud on the banks of the river and they flicker, disappearing and then reappearing, like the magical glitter on the scales of a fish. The shadows see the bits of our girl's boat, her boy's hotel pamphlets and the sweet wrappers, floating on the surface of the water. And they see the fishing wire; it is tied around her boy's foot, attached to the root of the willow tree, whose veins are fed by the deep black water. The other shadows see her boy flailing, his face is very red and angry; not a devil, really, just a disappointment, and then the shadows see him going still.

Our girl clings to her boy, her legs wrapping around his body, her arms circling his neck, and her eyes switching. The fishing wire keeps hold of her boy, and he seems to grow from the riverbed now, a tall plant, his clothes and hair billowing away from his body in the water. Our girl's shadow drapes carefully over our girl and falls against her, fingertip to fingertip, toe to toe, her shoulder blades are capped with a sheen, like dust, or something even lighter, it is water or sweat. Our girl feels a flip in her stomach, the thrusting kick of a frog in a blackened pond, twisted damp fingers on the black, dark hill. It is night-time now, but our girl looks around herself, eye-upon-eye-upon-eye, and she is sturdier; her eyes can see very far, through the pitch-blackness of the river. She can see the shadows thrashing, and she knows, as she swims towards the place where the river falls, an eel flickering through the waters, that the other shadows are putting their long strange fingers into the wood; they are poking at the cracks.

Sea God

Min's washing machine isn't working properly and she doesn't want to have someone in to fix it. She doesn't want strangers in the house; they might comment on her living space, how she hasn't got around to a proper clear-out, what things are there that shouldn't be. Min has a son, Crispin, but he is very busy. Crispin doesn't visit enough to notice Min's stink. Even so, Crispin is the only proper connection to her past, her stories, and Min wants to tell him about a memory that she found that morning, in the bathroom.

Min noticed one of Louie's cufflinks, hidden behind the neck of the sink and the stacks of old magazines and newspapers that she keeps in the bathroom, the crates full of empty toiletries, special old scents, spent shaving creams: the cufflink was a silvery mouse. There was a time when Min had kept the house very neat, pristine, but since her husband's death, bits and pieces; they will keep popping out on her like this. Without looking properly,

Min knows that this is one of the cufflinks that Louie wore on the boat that took them to their honeymoon on the Isle of Wight, that he wore the cufflinks with his blue suit and his buttercream shirt, and then the memory starts to play, as though projected on the mildewed wall.

There was a woman with very thin white hair, a salmon-pink scalp, and fidgeting hands; this woman had dropped her carpetbag over the side of the boat. In the memory, Min sees how the bag didn't sink, how it floated ridiculously on top of the grey waves, and how Louie had made such a fuss that the crew had actually agreed to stop the boat to retrieve it. The woman was very old, she had very thin hair – but even so, Louie had always been keen on damsels in distress. And when the carpetbag was hooked up, out of the water, its owner had already disappeared, hadn't she, and what they found inside ... *Well, you'd never guess what they found inside the bag.*

Min wants to share with her son, each time she gets a surprise like this, a memory so piercingly intense it feels as though she is possessed: the flash of Louie's hand on the quince-coloured rail of the ferry; the moles on his young jagged back, greasy with suncream; her own smudged face looking back at her from the tin mirror in the ferry toilet. But every time she tries to get started, Crispin is impatient even before she can find the right words. She can hear him walking around in his house in Plum Regis, where everything is absurdly clean and the walls are all painted the same colour, sighing: *Yes, I've already heard this one, M.*

After Min's mother had died, everyone in the family started calling her 'M', not just for Min, but also for

'Mother'. M made sure that things went on, just as they were supposed to. M was mother to everyone: Crispin, Louie, her sister and father, her nephew and even her little dog, Missy. M was always jumping from task to task, no time to sit or even stand still until suddenly, everyone was gone.

Min gets the answer machine. Crispin updates his message every time he is flying, so now she knows that he is in Nancy, somewhere in France, and that he'll be back on 13 March, which is in ten days' time. Min feels defeated by her son's voice, so flatly confident and booming, and she forgets about the phone charges, rambling on about her washing machine and the stink, about how he knows she likes to keep herself neat. She starts to tell Crispin the story, the cufflink and how it has reminded her of the ferry trip. Now Min is talking about the sea, the thin-haired woman and her clumsy hands, her bag that was full of— But the answer machine cuts her off and she is left with the sharp dialling tone.

This is the way things tend to be; Min is full of stories but they are kept, very quietly, inside. She has no one to talk to, and besides, she doesn't really know *how*. There is a plate from lunch on the side, next to bottles of prescription medication; some of this medication belongs to Min Dimorier, pills for her legs, which are threaded full of knobbly veins that throb and burn from standing and fetching and serving for nearly all of her life; some bottles are made out to Louie Dimorier for his blood pressure and his dermatitis; there are even bottles that had helped the little version of Crispin Dimorier when he needed to recover from whooping cough or an ear infection. Min only makes simple, boring meals for herself: functional food, to make her full, although she used to bake endlessly for other people: strawberry and rhubarb pie, cream cheese pound cake, coconut chiffon and angel food. One of the cupboards is full of old ingredients, cutters and jelly moulds, piping bags, ganaching plates and mixers. There are traces of ketchup on Min's discarded plate, floating inside the chip fat: red commas. Min puts her finger into the red sauce and licks the tangy taste.

Later that evening, Min gets a text message from Crispin:

> M, probably the filter. I'll order a new one and fit it when it comes. Let me know.

Min pushes through the junk in the front room, all bits and pieces accumulated from the department store and from her long life, all proof that she has existed, that there are things that Min Dimorier has done. There are sacks full of stockings, threaded together like worms, and Christmas decorations, tinsel and baubles, littered around the carpet with old dog toys, chews, and even some plastic bones in a corner. Crispin's school portraits aren't displayed on the walls, they are piled one on top of another, a tower of frames and missing teeth in different smiles. Black-eyed teddies cover an entire armchair and a marionette with a broken arm hangs from the front of the looming wardrobe; a dusty ornamental scene shows a miniature boy and a miniature girl skating across a glass lake. There is a large plastic rabbit whose paws hold an empty pot labelled 'GOODIES'. Min looks at the cufflink for a moment and then drops it into the rabbit's pot.

She tiptoes upstairs to bed.

Min gets the bus out of Clutter, she visits a launderette that she remembers, past Upper Skein and the Lilybank River, even past the doctor's surgery in Plum Regis and the other department store; it is far away from Paradise Block, but Min doesn't care. Min can't stand for too long, the veins in her legs hurt her, but she can easily walk from the bus stop to the launderette. She smells salt in the air and remembers that she is near the sea, where boats pass by. Inside the launderette, people are standing by their bags, patting their flanks and checking on them, zipping and unzipping, all their private items inside. There are girls wearing tops that show their long stomachs, the firm stretched skin of an animal: a deer or stag, the muscle so tight. These girls sit on top of the machines and shout across to each other, as if they can't stand to be quiet, not even for one moment.

Min thinks that the girls ought to stop their noise, that they ought to get their washing done and go home; she listens to the clothes thrashing around inside the drums and tries to ignore their voices, as they complain about their boyfriends or husbands, their children and friends, dropping coins noisily and whistling when a man comes into the little room. One of the women is pregnant and she talks about the baby's father still finding time to go down to The Brass Cross, finding time to cheat, even when there's no money for a cot, and even while she's like this, blown up like a balloon. The woman has very round eyes that remind Min of a shark and she's drawn all the way around them with a blue eyeliner.

'Just as soon as I can run,' shark-woman says, 'I'm going. I'm leaving that motherfucker.' And she takes off one shoe and starts massaging her foot, as though she is preparing for her escape already.

Min never complained about Louie like this. She remembers him coming home at two or three in the morning; the car parked over two spaces in front of Paradise Block, calling, 'M, get up and fry me some kippers.' There were bottles, scattered around the brakes of their car, the anonymous lipstick that had been lost in the soft leather folds of the front seat. *What a piece of rubbish he was, what a motherfucker*, she thinks, but she doesn't say. Min has always been quiet, keeping herself packed tightly inside; and now, in the launderette, she feels like she is spying on some very private scene, a man and a woman getting undressed; a terrible injury – a child weeping alongside a hospital bed. The vibrant sound that the women are making is deafening; when they go to unload their machines, their heels screech against the tiled floor, biting aggressively, and Min notices that her legs start to throb, even sitting down.

Min wouldn't usually make a visit to the beach; she is a very practical person, always busy. But now Min wants to burst out the door, get away from where the women are laughing and bitching, telling each other their stories; she wants to sit on the pebbles while she waits for her washing to be done. Min thinks about standing at the edge of the water and taking off her shoes and stockings, putting her purplish toes on the goblin stones.

It is on the beach, on this day, that Min sees the sea god.

The sea god has long, very green hair and a pierced lip on one side. He is not looking at her, but rather down at the beach, where his metal detector is hovering. Min watches him for a while, her eyes following him up and down the shore. Min likes the way the sea god is so intent on his searching, looking for things that can't be seen. While she follows the sea god with her eyes, the waves are crashing rhythmically behind him and Min is entranced: the water makes her think of the thin-haired old woman again, the oddities that the ferry crew had pulled out of her carpet bag, her glistening pink scalp. If Louie had let the bag rest on the waves it would have been turned over eventually, in the night or during a storm; it would have disintegrated over time, and maybe some of the contents would have found their way to shore, maybe to this exact beach, where the sea god could find them.

Min watches the sea god walking over cans; they collapse under his big boots.

By the time Min gets home the big laundry bag has scored a mark into her arm. She feels restless; the silence in her flat is close and the path that she takes from the kitchen to the bedroom is very worn and looks startling to her now. The carpet on the stairs is balding in the middle, and down the left-hand side of the bed there is the distinct trail where Min's sore feet have scuffled along. This carpet gives away the secrets of Min's routine.

Sitting at the table, Min realises that she wants to bake something, to make carefully iced cupcakes and sprinkle each one with little silver balls, but she has no one to bake for. Min feels her tummy gurgle and squirm. The washing machine is there, silent and moping, with its big black eye leaking a rusty tear. Min goes to the fridge and stands in its light; the smell of the food is intoxicating, but not delicious – something inside Min is saying, *No*, her feet and ankles throbbing, and she goes to close the door—

It is sunny on the beach, but Min hasn't brought lemonade or sandwiches. She has a whole tin full of marble cupcakes that she has made. The cakes are iced and she knows that there are chocolate shadows and whorls inside, because she has baked them herself. Min isn't used to eating much; she has never eaten for pleasure, but now she grabs a cake and stuffs it into her mouth, ignoring the silvery cake fork that she has brought with her. This fork came into Min's life on her wedding day, part of a set of silverware that she has polished and kept nice for all of these years. As an experiment, Min pokes the little fork in between two stones, sees how it looks there, shimmering like a piece of rubbish. The cake is very dry, and she struggles to chew it down, so that she can take another big bite.

There are five cakes left in the tin and Min crams one into her mouth. She chokes a little bit, but she eats it all. The sea god looks over and stares at her for a few seconds, as if he is trying to get her into focus. He raises his hand and waves.

The sea god's metal detector is attracted to a piece of tin foil that is near Min's foot. It is a drizzly day and they are the only two people on the beach. Min's limbs feel stiff from sitting on the stones and the cold air is creeping inside her raincoat, her ankles and calves are throbbing.

'That's just a piece of rubbish,' the sea god says.

Min sees the outline of the sea god's body underneath his damp T-shirt. She remembers her husband. She wants to ask the sea god whether he has found anything else, anything special, a surprise. Before Louie died, he told Min that he had a great surprise for her but that she'd have to wait until later, then she'd see. He was in the bathroom when she found him, clutching the comb that he'd been using on his hair. A bottle of aftershave had fallen on to its side and spilt its luminous green contents into the sink. Over the next few months, through the intensity of her mourning, Min had believed herself waiting for a surprise, but she could never uncover what it might have been, even when she looked through all the pages of Louie's diary and inside his pockets. Min was afraid that the surprise might have been his death, and whenever she looks at pictures of him now, she can hear him saying, *Made you jump, GOTCHA!*

Min feels a bubble inside her chest, her neck, and she says: 'Yes, just rubbish.'

Min sees the sea god; he is right there, talking to her. The way the sea god is standing, Min imagines him on the bow of a ship, his green hair whipping in the wind.

'That's the way it goes,' he says, smiling, and he waves goodbye, starts to move off again.

'Just a minute,' Min says. She is looking for something in her bag; she wants to offer the sea god something. She doesn't know why, but she needs to – messages, symbols passed, hand to hand, to hand.

Min can talk to the sea god this way.

'Here,' Min says. She unclips a brooch from underneath her rain jacket. The brooch had belonged to Min's sister; Min remembers it shimmering on her sister's trench coat, the shape of two cherries. The sea god sits down next to her to examine the brooch. He rubs the brooch with his thumb, as though he needs to remove some dirt. Min thinks that this rubbing is a habit because there is no dirt; she has kept the brooch nice.

'Well,' he says, 'I've never found one of these.'

Min wants to talk about her sister, where she had worn the brooch and how much she had liked it, but each time she opens her mouth, the sea is too loud and she cannot find the words.

'Would you like a cake?' Min asks.

Min sits with her feet together, and the sea god sits next to her.

There is a storm, plastic bags are whipping against lamp-posts on the street and the rain is slamming into the windows of the launderette. Min is scared to go to the beach; she thinks that the sea might swallow her, leave her umbrella and handbag bobbing on the surface of the water, her stockings twined amongst the black seaweed. She sits and waits, listening to the women and watching. There is a new baby in the launderette, but shark-woman isn't talking about running any more; she wears her stilettos and passes around a thick gold chain with a love heart weighing it down. The chain coils back into her hand. She talks about getting her figure back, as though her pre-baby body has wandered off somewhere, gracefully leaning between some shady trees, or posing in a shop front; and she nearly screams when another woman mentions a new diet that she's heard about, the Bone Plan.

The washing still smells musty when it is done and as Min folds it back into her bag, she realises that she has forgotten to add the cap of fabric conditioner. The fabric feels stiff against her skin; it is brittle, uncared for. As she leaves the laundrette, Min sees an old man with a giant stick of candyfloss; he is leaning heavily on a woman who wears red shoes. Some way out in front a young man, narrow-shouldered and still with freckles, shouts to them, and when the wind steals the words, he gestures, points down towards the sea. The woman is laughing uncontrollably as they sway this way and that, and Min wants to chase them, to reach out and slap the woman, who is shouting between her peals of laughter, 'Wait, don't leave me!' They head down the road that leads to the beach and Min narrates to herself, *They'll get in trouble, if they go down there; it's too windy, too windy by far.* She walks gingerly to the bus stop, glancing three, four times down the road that leads to the beach.

When Min gets home, she sees the washing machine part lying on the mat in the hallway. The part is too big to fit comfortably through her letterbox, so it has been forced through, and most of the envelope has come away. It is 22 March, so Crispin will be back from France, but somehow, Min doesn't want to see or even speak to him. Now Min has a secret that she doesn't want to share with Crispin. Min sits and looks at her washing machine, the brown tear that has leaked from its drum. It is strange, but Min doesn't know if she wants the washing machine to be fixed or broken; she thinks about the sea god, standing alone beside the grey sea.

Min doesn't have any washing to do; she has already taken all of her pillowcases and sheets down, the cushion covers, and a bag full of flannels that she found, even some of Crispin's old teddy bears, who came out of the drum with bright black eyes, but no matter, Min decides that she must go to the beach. This isn't the kind of thing that Min would usually do, but she does it anyway. She leaves Clutter, gets the bus all the way to the beach, and a few stops before she needs to get off, she sees an old-fashioned shellfish bar on the side of the road. The fish is displayed for tourists on the shoreline; and while the bus waits in traffic, Min can see the glistening purple and silver of oysters, the shimmer of fish scales. A man leans up against the side of the hut wearing wellington boots and orange waterproofs. Min is daydreaming: she remembers how much Louie liked fish, kippers, cod, salmon, tuna, bright white crab sticks, striped with red, and even skinny little sardines. She remembers his face when she had cooked him a pan of fish stew for his supper; *No, no, no,* she says, in her head, he didn't just *like* fish; he *loved* fish.

There is an old woman sitting next to Min and she turns to her. 'Excuse me?' she says, and Min realises that she has been murmuring to herself.

Min feels embarrassed and she doesn't want to look at the old woman.

She sits up very straight in her seat and says, 'Oh, nothing. I was just saying, my husband loved fish for his supper. Don't worry,' but the old woman is nodding, as if Min has made a simple comment about the weather.

'They do, don't they,' she says, 'these men.'

Min knows that this is a nonsense reply and she wants to tell the old woman that Louie didn't just like fish, he *loved* fish, he wanted fish on Christmas Day, instead of turkey; he loved fishing, cod, straight from the sea; but as she opens her mouth, she feels the words are inept, as though she is holding the fish in her hands, it wriggles out of her grip.

How can *fish* be enough to explain Louie to this old woman?

Min probes the inside pocket of her brain, but there are many irrelevant items there: forks and brooches, plastic rabbits, Bundt cake, dresses and suits, Christmas reindeer, cod, apple tart, weighing scales, ganaching plates; these are all symbols, but she cannot see properly what they represent. Everyone is gone. *Those fuckers have gone*, Min wants to say, but instead, she gets out her box of shortbread and offers one to the old woman. The shortbread squares are covered in very fine sugar and a snow falls on the woman's pleated skirt.

It is night-time and Min feels oppressed by many thoughts and memories, the room and the furniture seem tight and she thrashes around in the bed. She pictures washing machines turning endlessly and further on, at the beach, the tides crashing down on inert stones, the luminous fish slipping through the moonlit water.

Min lets her hand fall into the empty space beside her. When she was young, before she had met Louie and needed more time to care for the family, Min had trained as a dental nurse, silently passing different tools for drilling and tapping. She uses teeth to try to sleep, repeating the names until she has made her way around the whole mouth, when she starts again: *Second molar, first molar, canine, lateral incisor.* Min tries, but the tongue keeps dropping away and the teeth scatter down, inside a black hole. Instead, she remembers having a tooth pulled, in her early twenties, how she had been disgusted when the dentist showed her how far down the tooth had reached, how deep inside of her the tooth had been. *Second molar.* Min had wanted to keep the tooth but her boss hadn't let her. He had been stern, that dentist. That's how men were then. Min had imagined the tooth, alone in a bin somewhere, in amongst glowing pieces of tissue and dirty things. That tooth had been a part of Min and then it was gone. She tongues the gap in her mouth now, forty-nine years later.

Min keeps her eyes tightly shut against the shadows in the room, but in her mind she sees shark-woman with her pushchair; she is running in her yellow heels, chasing someone who wears a jacket that Louie used to own.

Min is grinding her teeth; she wants to speak, but she knows that the words will be frighteningly loud in the darkness. She stays quiet, but she does get up, out of bed, collects a bag from the back of her wardrobe; she doesn't need to turn the light on to feel exactly where the items that she needs are. Her fingers run over some cool mould that has begun to form on the surface of the bag; the back of her wardrobe must be getting damp.

In the front room it is even darker; there is only one

window letting streetlight in, but Min still doesn't want to turn on the light. Min opens her jewellery box, it snaps like a jaw; this is her expensive jewellery and she can see the glittering. Min pours the jewellery into the bag. There is a whole drawer full of old sunglasses, their arms laced together, and Min adds these before she moves to where she keeps Louie's things, the huge double-breasted wardrobe that Crispin has moved downstairs for her. It stands in the gloom like a tall man.

Min doesn't stub her toe or stumble, even with her bad legs, although this wardrobe is more difficult to open, because it has been years since she last looked inside. There is dust and Min coughs. Inside, Louie's possessions have been sleeping, all this time: a ring that his father gave him when he turned eighteen, inscribed with his initials, LD; a cigarette box that had only ever held the same six cigarettes, never smoked; and a letter-opener with a faux-ivory handle. She sees the silver comb that Louie had been clutching that day, when he had surprised her in the bathroom.

Min throws all the items into the bag, except for the sharp letter-opener, because she doesn't want the sea god to hurt himself. The last thing that she does is pull off her wedding ring, over the part of her finger that has turned knobbly and gnarled. She drops the ring into the bag and touches the naked space; the skin is clammy and new.

Min catches the very first bus to the beach and the sun rises, pale and gentle.

Min sees the sea god arriving at the beach. It is hot now and he is wearing a vest. The sea god is pleased to see Min and she stops smoothing her rug and fussing for a moment to wave back at him. She watches him intermittently as he bends down to examine the things that he has found. The pulse in her neck is thumping, and when Min sees that the sea god is coming over to where she is sitting, she busies herself with her cool box. Min is incredibly hungry, she has put on half a stone, but she cannot stop eating. She is ready to start on her rock cakes when the sea god is suddenly there, leaning on his metal detector. The sea god holds something; something is glimmering in his palm.

'What is that?' Min asks. She grasps the plate on her knees, she is clutching on to it tightly, as though the plate is the steering wheel of a car. Min wants to get rid of the sea god suddenly; she is shy, worried that the sea god will have one of Louie's cufflinks in his hand; her silver cake fork; her nephew's abandoned watch, with the black diamonds all around the face; the bug-eyed sunglasses that she wore on the Isle of Wight. The sound of the tide is brushing against the stones.

'I don't think there's anything good around here,' Min says, but the sea god ignores her. How could Min possibly know what was hiding under the stones?

'It's a gold tooth,' says the sea god, as if this is the simplest thing in the world. The sea god is grinning at Min.

'A tooth?' Min says.

The sea god is sitting down and he pats the stones next to him, asking Min to move closer. Min picks up the corner of her rug, moving all of her things over so that she can sit with the sea god. *She liked baking*, Min hears someone saying, would Crispin say that about her, after she had gone? *Min Dimorier never sat down; she baked like a mad bitch.* Min looks at her box: it is full of cakes that she has made.

'Imagine,' says the sea god. He is leaning into Min so that she can see properly. 'Someone walked around for a long time with this in their mouth.'

Min looks at the tooth now, the gold part is brown rather than gold, but it has little staggered steps in it, from chewing and gnawing at things. Min nods. The tooth intrigues her.

'Someone must have lost it,' Min says, staring at the tooth. 'A day at the seaside; a stick of rock.'

'Maybe true,' the sea god says. He is looking out into the waves, holding his hand open still. It is as though he is trying to receive a kind of message from the waves, and the tooth is his talisman.

Min looks curiously at the wet hairs in his armpit. The sea god is moist all over, but he has psoriasis on his elbows: the skin there is dry and scaly. Min touches her stockinged leg; underneath the stocking there is a huge tangle of green veins and sore grape-coloured skin.

'There's all sorts under the rocks,' the sea god tells Min, snapping out of his trance.

He moves his fair eyebrows around and reaches into his trouser pockets; Min sees that he is wearing her sister's brooch on one of his belt loops. 'Wedding rings,' he tells her, 'pendants, spoons, teeth, like this one. I found a dog collar; a photograph, a school portrait in a silver frame – the stones keep the treasures dry and they're there, just staring up at me. It's like I've uncovered a secret world, a bedroom dresser. I found a finger ...'

'A finger?' Min looks at the sea god sharply, she is munching on a rock cake, dry and crumbly between her teeth like sand; it falls from her lips. Min offers the box of cakes to the sea god and he takes one without looking – he doesn't care which one.

'A replacement finger,' the sea god says, chewing. 'You know? A prosthetic.'

Min nods and they are silent until the sea god takes one more item from his pocket, rubbing his thumb along the silver edge of a comb.

'M,' the sea god says, and Min jumps. She stares at the sea god, where he is pointing. 'Look,' he says, and Min sees the silver comb; a surprise, hidden inside the wardrobe: *M, I love you*, is engraved along the bow of the comb. The sea god rubs his thumb along the words, a habit that he has, and then he whips the comb away, back into his pocket.

'There's stories under these rocks,' the sea god says, and Min nods again. She sees one of Louie's cufflinks in the sea god's hand and the quince-coloured rail on the boat bound for the Isle of Wight; she thinks about the woman with the thin hair, her pink scalp and her carpetbag full of useless things: children's teeth and costume jewellery, small bones and bent spoons.

'Stories,' Min says. She brushes off her hands. Min touches the stones and they are warm. Before she picks up another cake, Min thinks about what is underneath.

Bad Elastic

Marie is twenty-one, and has been living with Shell for a year now, both in one tiny room in Paradise Block. Shell is the one who bosses Marie, even though she's only twenty-six herself; she tells Marie where she can and can't go, what she can do, especially when she can spend their money and how much. Shell has a baby in care, and she wants to get it back, goes on about it, all the time. There's a photo of the baby in a nice frame that Marie bought at the Clutter department store one day. All the nice touches in the room are because of Marie, really: the lacyish curtain, the antiquey-looking clothes rail, these sweet little ornaments along the windowsill. But Shell gets cold every time Marie buys even one small thing – she only cares, pretty much, about saving money so that they can get a flat with an extra room, prioritising the baby first and foremost, every time.

The baby isn't even that cute, potato-faced in Marie's nice frame. The photo that they have is very old, taken on one of those crappy android phones, and the baby's face is really just a smudge on the discoloured background. Marie puts her thumb and first finger over the baby's face, enough to blot it out of the room. Shell grunts and Marie takes her hand away quickly.

Shell is sleeping, even though it's their only day off together, even though she'd promised Marie they'd do something nice, go down to the department store and buy a very small thing, at least the soft ice cream with the red sauce, probably not a burger, because Shell said that they were vegetarians now, but maybe some sweets, liquorice or caramel. Marie is always nostalgic for the department store in Plum Regis, where she would shop for many small things with her mother and father, sometimes her spoilt little sister, Tamsin, and she likes to go down to the Clutter store, not to buy anything, just to walk around thinking about how different life is now that she is independent – living with Shell, like a pair of bandits, a pair of really real poor people, surviving all alone together.

But now Shell is snoring, thrashing around in their bed, and Marie feels depressed, despondent, and also sneaky. Marie has been thinking about a small thing, a dress that she has seen in the Clutter department store. Weeks ago she saw the dress, and now, weeks later, she is still thinking about it nearly night and day. It was like the dress had followed her home, enchanted and possessed her. Of course, Shell would tell her she was *not* enchanted, just spoilt; a brat who needed treats and tickles, and didn't want to work to pay for them. But Marie is only twenty-one; she only left her family a year earlier, and she still got little bits of money sent in the post along with tragic weepy notes from her mother. And she saves most of these bits of money, a lot of it; it all goes into the cereal box, all savings for Shell's baby. But not thinking about the baby night and day made Marie a brat, made Shell decide that they'd been raised differently, that she could never understand what it was really like to be Very Poor, even though Marie had left most of her nice things at home, her jewellery and her face creams that she liked to use, almost all her expensive dresses, even her favourite – the soft pink satin that she had worn when she had been crowned runner-up prom queen.

Marie stares hard at the lump that is Shell, a little tuft of hair showing bright against the greying pillows. Very Poor or not, she thinks, daring herself, Shell was the one who didn't have a single millisecond of common sense. Shell wouldn't even put their money into a proper bank account because she thought the evil bank people would steal from them somehow, and that's why all the money was hidden inside the cereal box, in the drawer, underneath the twisting mounds of tights and knickers, all of which had what Marie's mother would call 'bad elastic'. But now, and not for the first time, Marie sees an advert for a bank savings account on the television – a high-interest account, available to really any customers, and she leans in a little, sitting on the old chair that they have, wrapped in their fusty pearl-coloured blanket.

Use the great rate of interest to treat yourself, the television man is saying, *treat yourself to any small thing*.

Shell's leg spasms out of the bed, a thing that happens when she is dehydrated (and they had been out drinking at The Brass Cross all of the night before, and Shell had wanted them to sit out on the kerb and count their coins back into the purse, *after* they had spent most of the money on golden tequila and black wine and on pale, quite raw chips, which they fed into their mouths, and long, thin cigarettes, which they sucked on, very hard, right into the early hours of the morning). Shell moans and rolls over in the bed, whispers to Marie to bring her water in the big jug that they use, and then she is asleep again.

Marie tiptoes to the drawer, rummages underneath and amongst the bad elastic, stuffing the paper into her little velvet handbag, and then she is clip-clopping down the stairs, and out into the sunshine that is neatly folded around the greyness of Paradise Block.

There are boys outside, loitering, endlessly adjusting their trousers and kicking invisible dust on the pavement, and they follow Marie a little way down the road.

'Where's your friend?' one of the boys is saying. 'We wanna see you kiss her.' And Marie is laughing; they're so stupid, looking at her, drooling at Marie in her yellowdress.

She clip-clops a little faster, because she wants to get down to the department store, get the dress and easily pop the money into the high-interest savings account – *It's called using your common sense* – and she hears the concrete scuffling under the boys' trainers, the grumbling of their collective interest in her. Marie has no problem tossing her blondish hair over her left shoulder, holding the velvet bag full of money close to her side, feeling her yellowdress moving in the rhythm of her clip-clopping, the fabric on top of her solid flesh. But then, when Marie sees a whitish van, the words 'taxi car' on the side in sticky, peeling letters, she wants to get into it already, only a little way out of Box Close. If Shell was with her, she'd shout something cutting, bark at the boys – *Fuck off, go home and play with your little dicks* – but she isn't, and Marie is just too *nice*; she couldn't be so horrible and mean like Shell was, and maybe that was a good thing; (*Shell holding a man's neck in The Brass Cross, telling him to just try saying those rude words in front of her girlfriend, even one more time*). They were just idiot boys, boys with way too much time on their hands, doing their thing, and from the back seat of the taxi car, she gives them a little wave while they gesticulate, holding on to their crotches as if their dicks hurt from even the sight of Marie in her yellowdress.

The taxi-car driver is looking at Marie in the little mirror, and Marie smiles at him, very friendly, until she realises that he is waiting to hear where she wants to go, and she says, 'Oh, ha-ha; the department store please,' and the taxi-car driver pops his pink gum with a sharp crack. Marie isn't sure that he has even heard her, but they move off into traffic, and when they stop at the lights there is a thump-or-slap on the window, and Marie jumps stupidly. It is a grey-green circle, a slice of pickle that has been taken from a burger and flung at the window.

'Oh, ha-ha,' Marie repeats, 'a slice of pickle,' and the taxi-car driver looks at her again, still says nothing. Marie holds the bag on her knees, all full of the bad-elastic money, and watches the bloodish numbers that represent her fare ticking up and up. She is trying not to think of Shell planning out a corner of the new room where they are going to put the baby, and where Marie could decorate with an animal mosaic and glitter pens if she wanted to,

185

trying not to consider what Shell might say when she sees Marie wearing the lovely new dress, telling her that her yellowdress was fine in the first place, and why did she have to do that – why did she always have to be such a brat? – explaining to herself that the interest on the account would cover the price of the dress anyway, this one small thing that she wants and should have.

So absorbed is Marie, with these bloodish numbers, and with not thinking about Shell and her baby, but actually thinking about Shell anyway (*Shell after a heinous shift, long and caramel in the lozenge-shaped bath, coughing and falling back, exhausted, into the tepid water. Marie rubbing soap into Shell's tangled red hair, putting her fingers into the holes that were her collarbones, and going to the kitchenette to cook them something soaked in butter, sprayed with little curls of cream*), that she fails to realise that the taxi-car driver is not taking her to the Clutter department store, but to somewhere else entirely.

It is the Plum Regis department store, already miles past the boundaries of Clutter and the Lilybank River, all the way through Upper Skein.

Marie doesn't say anything, but the taxi-car driver speaks as if she had: 'You didn't say *which* department store.' He is smiling, shrugging, wide-eyed with his cleverness. 'I could've taken you even further,' he tells her, saintly like.

Marie feels the Plum Regis department store looming over her, sees herself in the reflection of the taxi-car window; her yellowdress is supposed to be cinched at the waist, but it is actually quite baggy there: bad elastic.

Marie hands the taxi-car driver the money stiffly, waits for her change. *If he thinks he's getting a tip*, she thinks, and then, *He's ripped you off; you've let this prick embarrass you.* These are things that Shell would say, but the taxi-car driver is already away, moving off into the silence that surrounds the Plum Regis department store.

The ceiling lights blink like lizard eyes, guiding Marie past some of her absolute favourite departments – Biscuits, Caramel Sweets, Lipgloss – although, truly, she *had* remembered chandeliers hanging from the ceiling, actually; hadn't she told Shell about the Plum Regis chandeliers, twinkly like stars? And about the Plum Regis staffers jumping out of departments to greet shoppers on the walkways? There was the very centre of the store, where the food court was, hundreds of little tables and chairs placed in exact distances from each other, indistinguishable from the food court in Clutter, now that she sees it again, even though, in Marie's memory, there had been giant, comfy chairs, staffers wearing white gloves that flew around like fat birds.

Marie's heels are clip-clopping especially loudly, and she sees smudges of her yellowdress in the glass when departments have shop fronts, noticing the extent of the bad elastic again, the rumour of her puffy belly, and then she is at the food court, the paper runners on the tables definitely a different colour to the paper runners in Clutter; they are purple, regal purple, that was one thing she could tell Shell. It must have been the actual food that was very different and special in Plum Regis, Marie thinks, using her common sense, tastier, certainly more expensive she sees now, not about to buy anything, just looking. Marie stands still; *is she hungry or not?* She can't be sure. She remembers the video of the baby cows being forced into a van and then into tiny plastic-looking sheds, a strange alien neighbourhood full of crying – and she remembers agreeing with Shell, saying, *Oh God, so cruel.*

But Marie has already spent all of that money on the taxi car, been tricked into that, ripped off; so now that she has come so far, already about to be chastised by Shell for not caring enough about her potato-faced baby, she may as well get a burger and be told off and guilty about the baby-motherless-cows as well. The burger is the cheapest thing on the menu, her favourite treat and just a small thing – why shouldn't she have it? The staffer brings it out to her, perfectly centred on one of the square red trays that they use, and Marie doesn't even wait for her to go away before she takes a giant bite.

The taste makes Marie's eyes water, even her heart begins to palpitate as she stuffs more into her mouth, pleasure making her forget her body, her Shell. But then Marie notices something, a movement at the dark innards of the kitchen, where the burger was made, where the staffers must still be standing. There, inside, she thinks there are white eyeballs, teeth flashing – she can hear whispering, laughter. And Marie sees herself in the glass, before she can change her expression: her embarrassingly eager, happy face, as if in sex, as if the burger is her lover – her desire for the burger looks sickening, honest and exposed. Marie chews, but the burger starts to taste strange, hot grease; it is tangy, where it wasn't before.

Marie puts the burger down, picks up the knife; she will

cut the burger into pieces and eat it with her fork; but as she delicately divides the remaining food, she starts to see it differently. The bun is flaking, like a layer of loose skin; and the tomato is watery red, the inside of a lip; as she cuts, she sees almost translucent lettuce traced across the jaundice-yellow cheese, like broken green veins. Marie can't work out how to portion up the food, how to stay sitting at the table when she can feel the eyes on her, on her longish legs, her yellowdress with the bad elastic, the way her stomach puffed.

The fun of the Plum Regis department store is starting to leak away from Marie; she is imagining Shell waking up, asking for the big jug that they have, for water, and realising Marie is gone. But now that Marie has been ripped off by the taxi-car driver, made it all the away to Plum Regis, paid more than she would have in Clutter for a disgusting burger, it is like she cannot leave. Marie's feet must stick to the plan, take her clip-clopping towards Dresses, exactly where she used to come with her mother or father, sometimes her spoilt little sister, Tamsin. This is where Marie had bought her prom dress, and where she now sees a staffer who looks familiar. The staffer is yanking at a tangled nest of hangers, the wire glistening through the plastic sides of the box, like she has her arm submerged in a tank full of small sharks.

And as she gets closer, Marie realises that this clear-eyed, very defined face, belongs to one of her sister's friends: it is little Vivien Holm. Marie smiles, walks a little faster: really, it *so* embarrassing to see Vivien; what would she even say to her, after all this time? Vivien had helped get Marie ready when it was her turn to go to prom. And prom was where Marie had worn the soft pink satin dress, and where she had looked so stunning that she had become runner-up prom queen, and although she hadn't received a crown, she had been given a gift card, which she had kept past its expiry in a small portrait frame. Vivien had got down on to the floor and painted Marie's toenails, holding each toe to stick transfers of flowers and little diamantés to each nail, giggling and loud and rushed, almost hysterical, because she was part of this ceremony, hysterical at the thought that later she might get the chance to help Marie with her hair, to run her stubby, bitten fingers through Marie's blondish tresses.

Marie is making her way to the back of Dresses, where Vivien is working on the hangers, but little and now bigger Vivien is squinting at Marie, who is smiling broadly, now less broadly, now just a bit, as Vivien's eyes travel up and down, pausing very obviously on the bad elastic. The little velvet bag full of money, that Marie really ought to have already taken down to the bank if she ever wanted to earn enough interest to pay for all these small things that she kept buying, is tapping on her hip, *tap tap tap*, like an old friend. Marie sees in Vivien's face that she doesn't know her, her round eyes, and hears in her voice – 'Can I help you, miss?' – that she doesn't even have an inkling, not even the faintest memory of carrying Marie's corsage with two hands, placing it on Marie's knees as though they were an altar.

Marie smooths her yellowdress again; surely she can't look *that* different?

But Vivien just wants to lead her down one aisle and then the next, lazily pinching fabric out of the ranks of glistening, wet-looking taffeta, beaded, fussy silhouettes, not bothered by Marie, not even looking at her, telling her about other women, fancy and famous women who had chosen to wear whatever dresses before her, at whatever time, and repeating strange and stupid names – *Innocence, Forever Love, Be Mine, The Promise* – and which dresses are limited edition, one of a kind, special, and how they are *very* expensive (pausing again to look at Marie's yellowdress). Marie had often told Shell stories about the Plum Regis store at bedtimes, while Shell braided her hair into lots of little plaits, oily ropes that slipped all over Marie, telling her about the departments and the dresses, the staffers who smiled and shone – but now Marie can see that the dresses are actually very similar to the ones in Clutter, only they have sillier names, and far higher price tags.

While Vivien collects dresses and ushers Marie into the changing room, Marie realises that she'd really like to go now, really doesn't want a dress from Plum Regis, and doesn't want Vivien to see her any more, perhaps not like this, in her well-loved yellowdress, the taste of sour meat still accusing her mouth. Marie should keep Vivien's memory of Marie runner-up prom queen intact; Marie should go. But Vivien already has her in the changing room, and her voice drones on, very professional actually, wanting Marie to know the materials, ingredients included in these dresses, what parts make you slimmer, help with 'problem areas'. Marie is trying to keep her head down, saying 'yes' and 'very nice', just wanting to go home; to rinse her mouth, to have Shell make up her face and to go down to The Brass Cross together, eat chips and drink black wine; and it is only in the mirror that Vivien fully looks at her, their eyes locking together like two animals about to fight, and Vivien, actually very pretty, really grown into herself, but also very thin, as though she barely meant to be there, says, 'Marie Perkins-White?'

There is another staffer called Pinkie. Pinkie sidles out from behind the curtain at the back of the department when Vivien yells her name. Before the curtain can fall back and into place, Marie sees that many more dresses hang there, pink, red, yellow, they are all bagged and they shine and even seem to drip like newly killed meats.

Vivien tells Pinkie, over and over, how this is Tamsin's sister, Marie Perkins-White; and there's Marie, half dressed, reaching out from behind the curtain that she has wrapped herself in, smoothing the curtain material over her stomach.

'My God,' Pinkie says, expressionless, clearly following Vivien's lead, holding her gloved hand to her mouth. Pinkie looks older than Vivien, although she isn't wrinkled; her eyes are set very still in her head, and they are dark, watchful and hungry. Marie, wondering whether Pinkie even knows her sister Tamsin, does a faux curtsey, still holding the curtain.

'I would never have recognised you,' Vivien says, and then hushed, in a reverential whisper, 'you look *so* different.'

Marie laughs; poor little now bigger Vivien, ogling Marie, taking her in, and she says, encouragingly, 'Well, so do you, Viv. So grown up.'

There is silence. Pinkie comes to stand next to Vivien,

her shoes squeaking on the lacquered floor. They look at Marie.

'Well, okay,' Vivien says finally. 'Let's get you a really, really nice dress.' She is grinning now. 'Marie Perkins-White.' Shaking her head. 'A really nice dress,' she repeats. 'I've got a few favourites this season, a couple that would really suit you. It's all about learning your shape.'

And Marie nods, even though she wants to laugh, Vivien Holm giving *her* fashion tips? Now *that* was stupid. But really, shouldn't she get going anyway? She ought to get down to the bank, using her common sense, get the bad-elastic money into a high-interest account for Shell's baby, especially since the dresses were so much more expensive here, in Plum Regis.

'And you can use my VIP discount card,' Vivien says, as if reading Marie's mind, proudly showing Marie, her name and grinning photo printed on the silver plastic. Pinkie takes her card from a pocket in her uniform, shows Marie too – and they stand there like that for a few moments, a stalemate, until Marie says, 'That's really nice, thank you.'

Marie does try to break out of the changing room, making herself part of the giggling that seems incessant, but Pinkie bars her exit with a watery blank smile, her very dark eyes glistening, and when dresses are thrust through the curtain, Marie accepts them, thinking, only a little bit panicky, about what Shell would say if she could see her, trapped by these two silly girls.

Vivien is saying, 'We'll help you, won't we, Pinkie?' as if Marie is a confused little creature who needed saving. Marie is finding it ridiculous, rolling her eyes when they aren't looking, and wrenching her body in and out of dresses, a seething rash of hives appearing on her breastbone, matched very closely by the pink organza that was next, pearls sewn all the way to the neck like they wanted to creep up and on to her cheeks.

Vivien and Pinkie sigh, murmuring, their brows furrowed, Vivien shaking her head, Pinkie sometimes laughing erratically at a joke that must have been whispered, too quiet to hear. And for some reason, Marie starts to feel tearful, as if she wasn't the one who had gone into the world on her own, to prove herself and live with Shell, without any money, learning on the job, every day, not having anything, no dresses, no burgers, no special face creams. And then it's as if the image of herself in Vivien Holm's small and mean consciousness shattering and disappearing like it had never existed is more painful than anything Marie has ever felt, more painful than Shell collecting vouchers, pennies from the creases in bus seats, shoplifting tampons, begging free drinks from old men, and swiping out-of-date packets of crisps from The Brass Cross.

But when Marie says that she wants to go, that she ought to, she's got to go to the bank, and she's not sure about any of the dresses, actually – they're not her style any more (but what is Marie's style? *Marie waving to her mother and sister, little Vivien Holm, grinning from the back seat of a real limousine, long and sleek, like a glistening eel*), Vivien grabs hold of her, eyes shining. 'I've had the *best* idea,' she says.

Marie stands in the soft pink satin dress, her old prom dress. It is identical and she realises that the seasons in

Dresses must be the same, every year they must just rotate the stock, transported from one back room to another, between department stores across the country. This would mean that the dresses weren't special at all. The fabric is very tight on her stomach, the place where Shell will use her fingers to tiptoe over the flesh; unexpected, she will push her face into the dough and blow raspberries that leave greasy heart-shaped smudges of lipstick; and Marie turns this way and that, smiling nervously at her reflection. Her skin is burning and she waits for Vivien or Pinkie to say something, even anything. Vivien struggles theatrically with the zip at the back, gives up, breathing heavily. 'Phew,' she says, and Marie goes, 'I quite like it with the back open, actually,' and Vivien smiles, nodding exaggeratedly, while Pinkie, staring blankly, says, 'It's too small,' and Vivien hisses, '*Pinkie!*'

When Marie turns side on, she sees that the dress has pushed her stomach into three different rolls, one that sticks out almost as far as her breasts, which are coming out of the side of the dress, as well as the top, even without the back being closed, and her eyes start to glisten while Vivien says, smiling sweetly, 'Never mind, I'm sure there's something else. It's a very expensive dress anyway, and you've worn it before, after all.' And instead of saying, *No, I've got to go, got to get the money into the high-interest account for Shell's baby*, and, *Get out of my way, you little idiot*, Marie hears herself saying, 'I love it, actually. I'll take it.' She marches out of the changing room, the soft satin pink dress swishing, swatting away Vivien's discount card, which comes towards her like a blade, and pours all of the bad-elastic money on to the counter.

Marie clip-clops along the long corridor, giddy; she wants to catch someone's eye, to tell someone what she has done, explode the story, but everyone is staring at their feet or into department displays, towers of toothy soaps or White Fingers biscuits, a gathering of strange mannequin children wearing boating outfits. Marie thinks that she will go to the toilet, change into her old yellowdress, with the bad elastic, but when she finds her way to the cramped, beige stalls, her yellowdress looks tiny and dishevelled in the bag. She can't figure out how the yellowdress had ever covered enough of her, and the new dress is swishing this way and that, hard to get off, because of the eyelets and the corset, hard to fit into the bag anyway, so she keeps it on, thinks that she will turn up at home wearing the dress, give Shell a fright and a laugh, tell her up front that she is going to return it the very next day anyway, and that she just had to show some stupid idiot girls something.

Marie clip-clops down the side of the store, where the buses and the taxi cars bring people and take them away. She sees a homeless woman, two left-footed shoes on her feet, one side of her spectacles smashed, and underneath there is the solemnly staring glass eye. A long grey crutch reaches down her side, wrapped over with ribbons and pieces of colourful material, some bells. Bottles of honey wine are strewn around.

She is excited to see Marie and she says, 'Oh, miss, Miss. Pink, in the beautiful dress! Beautiful, miss! Spare some change for a down-and-out.' And she waves her crutch around, obviously not able to stand up.

Marie digs in her bag for a bit of change, hand closing over a 50p, when she realises that this homeless woman is probably thinking she really is a very wealthy girl, shopping in Plum Regis, carrying a little velvet bag full of money (although she is careful not to let the woman see the money in the bag, the very much reduced amount of money), and she smiles at this homeless woman, down on her luck. The homeless woman can see Marie, the runner-up prom queen, Marie who hasn't changed so much in only a couple of years. She is about to explain how she's just wearing this dress because some idiot girls were jealous, made her try on all these dresses; and how she's going to return it tomorrow and take the money back – but then she decides, *Who cares?* She doesn't have to tell this woman anything; maybe she *is* rich, maybe poor, maybe Shell was the brat, not Marie, and Marie takes a £10 note jubilantly from the little bag and hands it to the homeless woman, her real eye popping with delight, and Marie clip-clopping the other way before she can hear the woman properly, 'Oh, thank you, miss!' starting to cry, blowing her nose so loudly, calling after her, 'Pinkie, oh Pinkie ...'

Marie can still see the Plum Regis department store in the distance, looming like a storm cloud on the horizon, but she has clip-clopped down several wide streets, now some littler ones, and she needs to get her bearings. There are taxi cars on the main road, but Marie thinks about the bloodish numbers ticking up with every blink, the £10 note that she has already given to the homeless woman. Marie would explain to Shell that she didn't even want this dress, that she had only bought it because her sister's old school friend had been jealous of her, patronising her, and she had wanted to prove – and slowly things begin to come loose in her head, and she begins to wonder why she *had* bought the dress, what the returns policy was, anyway. Marie wants to check the receipt in the little velvet bag, but she also thinks that what's done is done and she has her head held high, tough like Shell, but also stupid like, like *who*?

There are houses now, and somewhere, inside, a baby is screeching very loudly. Marie tries to look into the dark, flickering windows to where she hopes the baby is being rocked. Standing there, Marie feels a sudden, spontaneous sadness, a guilty taste in her mouth. Inside the new dress, Marie realises that she doesn't feel like Shell, *or* like herself, not a vegetarian, or a mother, a prom queen or a poor person bandit. There are cracks all over this street and Marie feels like she might dissolve and run damply down the gaps, and then Shell would never even know where she had gone. In the distance there is an unlit park, jagged branches of metal that represent a climbing frame, a set of monkey bars; Marie can just make out a swing that is moving in the breeze.

The new dress is against Marie, as she tries to creep back to the main road, past an alleyway where she can see a group of boys. She thinks that these might be the same boys that she had seen earlier, but she knows that they can't be, not really. There are gangs of boys all over, even in Plum Regis; they aren't waiting for her.

If Shell was there, she would shout out – *All right, lads?* – and they'd shout something back. Shell is like that: *but what is Marie like, though?* She opens and closes her mouth, but it is just air.

Marie wants to walk faster, because she sees that the boys are spilling out of the alleyway, creeping along by the walls of these front gardens that line the road, full of dead plants, stumps of cut-down trees; abandoned toys, plastic model aeroplanes and some dolls, reminders of disappeared children. Marie knows that the boys won't give her any real trouble, but still, she feels a little bit afraid, only in a silly way. She hears the sound of their trainers scuffing through the gravel to where she is clip-clopping towards the main road again, and then one shouts, 'Hey, lady,' and Marie has to stop, because they are coming out from behind cars up ahead and from behind and now they surround her.

There is a leader in the group. He has a handsome firm face, floppy hair. He keeps looking at his phone and scratching himself, like he doesn't care whether Marie is there or not, like he doesn't see her; but when she tries to push through the two boys at the mouth of the group, he just has to gesture and they stop her. The leader tugs on a joint, and little sparkles of fire fall over his fingers. Marie sees that he has very short fingernails and, instead of panicking, she wonders whether he bites them.

'What you doing out here?' he asks Marie, and then he adds, 'Nice girl like you,' and Marie tries to pretend that she feels the tension popping inside her chest.

'Oh,' she says, laughing. She grabs a handful of her dress, showing her disdain for the satin. 'I'm not ...' she starts. 'This little bitch—' Marie pushes the dress this way and that. 'She made me buy this dress.'

Marie tells herself that she doesn't feel scared; she feels embarrassed, she doesn't want the boys to see her like this, it is like they are seeing her naked, like they know the truth about Marie; and when Marie tries to remind herself of the little room that she and Shell share, the image that she sees is Vivien Holm again, rubbing shimmering lotion into her calves.

Marie wants to show with her voice, how she lives in Paradise Block, in one room with Shell. Marie is Very Poor, she doesn't have anything, not even one small thing, and Shell even has a baby in care; but as she thinks all of this, she compulsively pulls her velvet bag up to her chest, protecting it, like a child, a small animal, and the boys see it then.

The bag is gone, and Marie has fallen down so there is a stain on the new pink dress; it bleeds up from the bottom of the fabric, like an octopus spreading its tentacles, ready to spring back, tight and tiny into a dark black hole. Marie feels the absence of the little bag, and as she runs away there is a stitch, a pain in her stomach, as though something has been taken from her insides, too. Marie feels the loss of Shell's child for the first time. There is a mark, a slash or a semi-colon, and it doesn't signify anything except for a breach, the place where there isn't a something that should be there.

Back in Paradise Block, Shell is only just waking up and seeing the empty room. Shell stands at the window, looking at the powder pink in the clouds, which is being smothered by the dark inky blue that is fingering the horizon. Shell is eating a piece of apple with some cheese; this is a snack that Marie likes. These strange things, bits of knowledge that Marie holds, they impress Shell; how she will buy real cream for coffee, maraschino cherries to garnish their cheap vodka cocktails; the way she trusts; she will accept favours casually, she believes that people will be kind. She even enjoys the stories that Marie tells about Plum Regis; how everything is so different there, belonging to Marie and the strange world of her past self. Marie is trying to close that world down, Shell thinks, but things keep getting out; Marie can't hide these things for ever. Shell toys with a pile of change that Marie has discarded on the windowsill; it is enough for three pots of baby food, or ten cigarettes.

Shell stands at the curtain, without checking the drawer, the drawer full of the lady things, bad elastic; Shell knows that the cornflakes box is empty now. She stands at the window, waiting, hopping from foot to foot; she is fidgety, worrying skin on her lips with her fingernails; she picks up the little glass bell that is on the sill. The bell can't ring because the chime inside is moulded from a tonsil of glass and doesn't move. This is one of the useless things that Marie has bought to decorate their room and Shell turns it over and over in her palm, thinking about Marie and the way that she had tried to make Shell a special dinner, how Shell had yelled at her, 'That's a week's food money!' Shell goes to the dresser, pulls out a pair of her old knickers and finds the little pair of nail scissors that they have, carefully cutting the knickers into strips that leap into coils, even with the bad elastic. She picks up the bell, wraps it in the fabric, rubs her thumb over all of its parts until it is warm;

then she takes the little rabbit figurine, strange-eyed and droopy-eared, does the same thing. The glassy dolphin comes up the nicest, glistening wetly when a car passes and flashes light into the room.

When Shell finally sees Marie, she is wafting across the car park in a giant pink dress, limping and stumbling, a jellyfish; she wafts from side to side like she could be made of cloud or sea foam. Shell wonders what it would feel like to be that light, to have so little holding you down, until she can see from the way her shoulders are bunched that Marie is crying.

Shell keeps going to the door and turning the handle, then back to the window so that she can watch Marie safely across the stretch of concrete. She knows that she will hold Marie when she gets through the door; lose her hands in her hair and whisper into her ears, turn the little golden earrings that live in her lobes. Shell and Marie have lived side by side; their lives are twisted together now. And she wills Marie closer, past the troll trees that stretch their fingers into the dark, the occasional white cat that streaks across the grey like a comet: 'Come on,' Shell whispers, 'come on, baby.'

John's Bride

I am Annie, a good wife and woman with skills in cooking and cleaning, and in sensuality.

This is my story of the broken heart.

We were married on a Tuesday, when John was in full health and the sky was murky, white and pink, like the soft belly of a speckled rodent.

John said, 'Annie, we will be very happy. I can tell,' and then he held on to me, and his hands were all around my body. John licked his nice soft lips for me to kiss.

The guests were watching us, at The Brass Cross, and even though I didn't have very much English, and I did not yet know these faces, I repeated, 'Very happy,' and John held up my arm, like I had just won at a football match.

John said, 'Will ya listen to that, then? She says she's very happy!' and all of the people sprang out of their chairs clapping. Those were the words that the people had been waiting to hear.

There was no sadness on this treasured day, except

when we left The Brass Cross, and John fell down on to the floor and ripped a small part of my white dress.

John was spluttering, 'Anya, fuckin' 'ell, help me up, Anya,' and I looked down on him in amongst the cigarette butts and the bits of glass that shimmered like romantic stars in the sky, and I said, 'That is no longer my name, babylove. My name is Annie, Annie Dodd.'

But John, my babylove, he was laughing strangely, and saying, 'Anya Kolesnik, very thick, ha-ha-ha,' and even though I had not seen John light a cigarette, he suddenly blew out some smoke, which quickly disappeared, or was sucked back in, like silk, or a lizard tongue.

John had a very good job as a caretaker in Paradise Block, the same building that we lived in. But even though I wrote to Mama to tell her all about his work and his motivation, it was a bad situation, not good, because John told me that he had a big pressure with having to fix up the whole of the block by himself. The building was built very cheaply, with windows that will fall out, and damp and mould as thick as fur, a cat ghost creature that would slink into each and every flat.

I was so soothing and I asked John, 'Why don't you have a different job, or you could retire and get a state pension in two, maybe three years? Then we would spend more time, we could visit the English countryside, the green hills.'

This is what we had talked about before I came to Paradise Block, the promises that we had made.

But John said, 'I've got to keep you now. I'll be workin' till I die, just to keep you happy.' And then he got very angry, picking up a heeled shoe and throwing it across the room, saying about burdens and how things were different in the United Kingdom, especially where we lived, in Clutter, then accusing me of wanting to live in another place called Plum Regis. John said that he was married to Paradise Block as well as being married to me; there were so many sacrifices that he had made, and he could not be taking me to countryside parks, the places that I particularly wanted to go, because he had no car, and it was to cost an arm and a leg on the bus.

It seems so soon in our marriage, but this was the time that John began to tell me about the big pain in his chest, a knife stabbing, over and over, even though he was young, only sixty-four years of age, and about how this added to the pressure on his mind. John didn't want me to be worrying, so when I wanted to help, he would tell me to be quiet: 'Shut up! Shut up!' he would yell.

I told Mama that John didn't want to put a strain on me.

All the same, it was only a few years in the past, when I was still Anya, living in my little yellow-white room, that Mama had watched my tato die slowly, caring for him and with no thanks – washing in the bath and changing his clothes, even his underpants. He was ill for a long time, turning first red, cracked and sore-looking, like a stubbed toe, then seaweed-green, shuddering in the corner where Mama kept him, until finally he was blue: dead.

'John!' I would say. 'Please, won't you stay with me, where I can preserve your precious health?'

But John couldn't stay right by my side, because he had to work; every single day, and then he had to go and visit The Brass Cross again, to take away the stress of his existence.

Of course, in my mind I wasn't making a problem, but John said that I was a problem without even trying because when he would come home, I would be sitting in the front room with the lights off, like a fucking ghost, sitting there and giving him the creeps. But, and I didn't even tell my John this, I had not been out all day long and not even spoken to anybody, except a woman who had rung to tell me to buy an insurance package, and I just wanted to see my babylove and be close. (It is a secret that I spoke to the nice insurance woman about John's chest pain and all of my worries. I spoke to her for such a long time that I ended up giving her the long number across John's credit card.)

Anyhow, it was late and dark and I didn't want to worry John, so I just said, 'I thought you might like for me to wait up for you.'

I showed John some of my breasts by pulling down the pretty nightgown that Mama had bought for me, for my wedding night. The nightgown was especially for sensual purposes and very pretty, but Mama had been sad while she was watching me unwrap the pink tissue paper.

That was when John said to me, 'What is wrong with you, woman?'

And then John fell on to the sofa, wheezing and clutching his chest, and I saw that now, even my sensuality could cause a risk to John's health, and I immediately left the room, packing my gown away in a trunk while I listened to John's strange choking sounds, watching his lumbering shape through the cloudy glass in the bedroom door. I decided that I would put everything that could kill John into this trunk. John did not like me to have secrets, but I knew that this was for his own good, and I kept the key on a little chain around my wrist. For now, it was just the gown; so delicate and pink in the darkness, a dangerous jellyfish, floating in a black sea.

I held John's hand during the examination. I could see that he was frightened, that he was scared of his death, just as my tato had been.

The doctor wore soft plastic gloves and constantly wrote things on his computer. He wore a white jacket with three pens, red, green and blue, in his top pocket.

The doctor said, 'This is very *serious,* John. If you don't make changes to your lifestyle, you'll be in *serious* trouble within six weeks.'

I gasped in horror and repeated what the doctor had said: 'Six weeks!'

John turned to me and said, 'Shut it,' and then he turned to the doctor and said, 'I'm not even ill. I'm just stressed. I'm under a lot of pressure. It's just me, fixin' a whole block of flats, no one to help.'

John was pulling at his shirt collar as if it were too tight. 'Fifty-odd flats, I've got,' he carried on, 'and all of them with their plumbing goin', goin', gone. The walls are bustin' their own plaster; I don't even know how they're doing it. Every day, I've been getting a call from someone: "My ceiling's coming down on my baby's head, my water pipe burst on all my best clothes ..."'

The way John was talking, I was imagining Paradise Block as a terrifying sea animal, twisting all of its parts from one shape to another and bursting in and out of the dark water. John was sailing on a little ship that was like the death trunk, and on the shoreline was the green English countryside. I stood there, shouting into the black waves, 'Look out, babylove!'

'I'm sure I couldn't do it,' said the doctor, very respectfully, but John just scowled.

'I'm sure you could not,' he said bitterly. 'It's all very well when you're safe in your nice fancy office, you know.' He was pulling his collar again. 'Is it fuckin' hot in here or what? You're not saving on your heating bill, that's for sure.'

John kept talking over this doctor's head, to the wall with the poster that showed a healthy heart next to the unhealthy heart.

'I'm not ill,' John repeated, 'my heart looks like that one, not that one.' John gestured at the wall. 'You're using fear tactics to control me,' he added.

The doctor looked surprised. 'I know this must be a strain on you, John,' he said, 'but I have to tell you, being ill does not mean that you're a weak person.' The doctor smiled with encouragement. 'And you've got a lovely wife to look after you.'

I said, 'Yes, John,' very quickly, trying to hide the fact that I had been staring at the doctor's pens in his top pocket: Red, green, blue. *I had been thinking about my nightgown in the darkness of the death trunk.* And then I looked at John's face, which was turning pink around the edges.

'We can start by implementing a few changes to your lifestyle,' the doctor said.

He got up and started to look through some leaflets that were displayed next to the good vs. bad heart on the wall. John looked small and so sad, like a little boy in his smart shirt. He had been standing over me at home, saying to me while I ironed, 'Make sure you get all the creases.' I didn't know why he needed to be looking so smart for this little health visit in Plum Regis, but then, when we got on to the bus, I saw that John had even done up his top button and that he was combing his hair behind his ears with his big hands. I realised that my John wanted to impress the doctor.

But then, when the doctor began to talk about diets and vegetables, John started shouting straight away.

'What do you fuckin' know?' John yelled. 'My ma smoked till she was eighty-five and ate whatever the fuck she wanted. She had no problems! I can't be doin' with this, I want a proper doctor!'

The surgery door was on special hinges so it didn't slam like the doors do at home.

I sat with the doctor for a few moments, feeling very uncomfortable. How could John only have six weeks left? I was trying to calm myself; there was no need to get too excited and worried; maybe this really wasn't a *proper* doctor, but a fake, assisting doctor. He must know that surely John couldn't die this easily? John was solid and strong, like a lovely safe enclosure that I was to live inside for ever. In my head, I was standing inside of the death trunk, wearing the dangerous jellyfish gown.

'Listen,' said this doctor. I must have been looking very upset because he put his plastic hand on mine; he had not yet taken off his gloves. 'Maybe you could make some changes for John. It's not too difficult. Do you cook?'

'Cooking is one of my special interests,' I said, nodding.

I was thinking fondly of the little kitchen where I was cooking all of the time. Mama was working on training me to make foods when she heard that I was to be married to an English man named John Dodd who lived in a magical place called Paradise Block. She would show me the plate. 'You think this is good enough for Mr Dodd? The English gentleman?'

Then Mama would laugh cruelly and make me start again and even again until the dish was looking perfect, when she would cry and tell me, *Don't go, you can stay here and work in the local restaurant.* It was a shame that John only wanted Chinese takeaway meals and things from the microwave.

'Well, what John really needs is less fat, less red meat, less salt, and no sweets or crisps, desserts, etc. Do you see?'

The doctor handed me a little leaflet with all the foods that John was not allowed. All of the foods were looking delicious for John.

'I see,' I said, studying the foods and trying to memorise them, these were the foods that would make John die. I would have to be so careful!

'You can take these leaflets away with you,' said the doctor, reading my mind. 'And we really want to reduce John's alcohol intake, so if you could encourage him to stay at home, maybe have a weaker lager if he does have to drink.'

'The alcohol intake could kill John,' I repeated.

'And any stress you can remove, if John can get away with doing less overtime, that would be a really good idea,' said the doctor. His face was sincere. 'He says that he's maintaining a whole block of flats?'

My phone started ringing in my bag and I knew that it would be John, feeling angry in the car park.

I said very quickly, to confirm, 'Are you a doctor?'

'Yes, I am a doctor,' said the doctor, looking as if something was funny. The doctor took off his plastic gloves and made himself busy to hide his smiling. I saw that he had very nice clean nails and no wedding band.

'And you're sure all of these things will make John more sick? You have forgotten nothing?'

I fanned out the little leaflets that he had given me to make sure he could see them all.

'That's right,' said the doctor, and now he put his naked hand on mine. 'I'm sure that with the right support at home, John can reverse some of the damage that has already been done.'

'Thank you,' I said, smiling brightly at the doctor, but then my smile went away because the doctor was watching me, and it was then that I realised there was something really wrong with my John, and every part of my body cried out, Oh no! Would John be taken from me? Where could I go to live then? Would I have to return home and show Mama my failure, that she had been right all along? And whom could I love with all of my heart?

Outside, it had started to rain and the room got dark. I watched the raindrops on the glass for a moment with the doctor, both of us standing up, almost side by side. There was a tree and already the water was dripping from the leaves. I saw that the wet tree was dark black, holding out its arms, like a man wanting to grab something from the air.

'Look after yourself, Mrs Dodd,' the doctor said, very softly, 'you'll get wet.'

The doctor smiled at me in a strange way, and then the smile fell down and he sat in his chair and got close to his screen, typing words very fast. When he looked up again he was surprised-looking that I was still there.

I tried to stop John from going to the pub that same evening, but he just said, 'No woman will ever control me,' and he was off again, running through the rain that was silver. The rain was falling so heavily that I was seeing John in quick flashes, as though these droplets were parting for him like curtains, all the way to The Brass Cross.

While John was gone, I was angry, but I soon calmed myself by doing some searching on the computer. This was the computer that John had been using to talk to me, before I came to Paradise Block, talking all about how great our shared life would be; making the promises that he was sure he would keep. I looked for information about heart problems, and the things that could kill my babylove, and I searched for some other legal things about marriage to be practical, the terms and conditions for the insurance that I had taken out. And then, just for myself, I wrote, 'What does heartbreak feel like?' because I wanted to know, just in case the worst thing imaginable was going to happen, and I would have to act as the grieving widow.

I hid the leaflets very carefully in the trunk, as well as the letters that had arrived from the insurance company, and went to look in the kitchen cupboards, marking each sack of doughnuts, the packets of White Fingers biscuits, each tube of blood pudding and every tin of super-strength lager, with a small black heart.

There was a gas leak in the building, and John was out every day for so long. He said that lives depended on him and I told him, But John, what about *your* life! I kept expecting to see green smog coming under the door and filling the flat, but it did not happen. When John came back every night, he looked grey under the electrical light, but I knew that if I saw him in the daylight he would be looking green.

Seaweed, my John was drowning!

I had already tried to tempt John with all of the dishes that I had eaten and looked forward to on the special occasions when I was a child: there was borscht, prepared with duck, beef meat and veal; pampushki, the soft little rolls with the surprise cherries inside; and even kholodet, the delicious meat jelly that I had always savoured. But John said that he did not enjoy any of these dishes, he would rather have what he knew about already; the dishes that I made were too foreign and so weird, even though I had seen him greedily eating a Chinese takeaway very recently. So I decided that I would try one more food then, *for John's last chance*. It was to be stuffed squid, a Chinese-style dish that Mama had taught to me. The dish was made from fine baby squid, stuffed with pork and pickled vegetables, a delectable and tricky meal. This became one of my poor tato's very favourite dishes, so delicious; I remembered how pleased he was when Mama had cooked it for him, those mossy teeth he showed.

I had to place most of the items on order from the meat department, where the butcher looked at me very suspicious, and I was thinking that he would not serve me at all. The butcher wears a bloody apron and has a tattoo that says '100% British Beef' on his arm, which always makes me think that he may cut into his own flesh when I make an order of some steaks. When the bell rings, the butcher comes from behind his plastic curtains and looks at me. Before the plastic falls back into position, I can see where he sits on a deckchair and watches a small television, which is positioned on top of a metal cabinet. The butcher takes up my shopping list and looks with more suspicion, holding the list between his forefinger and his thumb. This is where I have learnt to take out John's credit card and place it silently on the counter.

I spent the morning chopping the pickled vegetables, the slimy grey mushrooms, looking a little bit alike to the death cap mushrooms that Mama used to collect to grind into powder for the killing of rats and other things. The colour of the mushrooms changed when I began to cook, and then they looked very pale, like blind eyeballs or snails. There were two more jars now, gherkins swimming in green water, like sleeping crocodiles, and leaves of cabbage that had become thin, nearly like wings or the skirt of an angel.

When the sun had moved to the other side of the kitchen, I looked at the clock and wiped the juice of the mushrooms on to my apron, pouring the red meat into a hot pan. The fat started to screech when it hit the oil, and for a moment I was frightened, but I quickly calmed myself – this screeching just meant that the oil was nice and hot, ready for the meat. I took out the squid. This part of the recipe was the biggest challenge and where Mama had always shouted, 'You see! You're not fit to be any old man's wife!'

Mama liked to hit the back of my hands with her wooden

214

spoon – *Don't go*, she would say, *please don't go!* – and then she would talk to me foolish lies, about how we could both get better jobs, have money to decorate, or even move to a bigger place with some money from a rich relative that might come. Poor Mama, her life was not arranged in her own hands.

I cut away the little squid legs, slightly greenish, reminding me of Mama's varicose veins; they stood out, so angry and proud. Mama said that those veins came from carrying me around when I was a baby inside, they were all kinds of sharp angles, but so delicate when you touched them, like the tubes of a heart. I had some marks of my own now, I had seen that there would be some very faint lines around my eyes – in some years these would be carved into my face, set for ever – but never mind, vanity was not so much of a matter to me. What mattered now was that I would treat these squid with as much care as I would treat John's heart, and then I would make the perfect dish.

There were eight squid, because I knew my John babylove to have the biggest appetite when he was coming back from work. Here was the first, which I picked up with my tongs and crouched over, pushing my finger inside the plastic seacave; it was bouncy, and I was cleaning out some bits of sticky plasma. Holding my breath, I lifted the squid a little higher and, with my face underneath it, I poked at the end with a single toothpick until there was a hole, so that the vegetables could breathe inside and didn't become a mess of sludge.

Next, it was a time for the stuffing, the most delicate part, and I turned off the radio so that I could concentrate very fully.

So strangely, I was thinking of Mama again; she was saying to me, 'This man will not love you! He will treat you badly! Like a dog!'

I felt my hand shaking as I put the first portion of pork and vegetable into the squid's body, and then I kept having to look behind me, into the room that was there, perfectly normal.

I was thinking that the meat was piping flawlessly into the plastic-like body and then the squid was escalating neatly around it, a little lung, when suddenly, the pod burst, and the meat began pouring out of the tear, hot and wet, and I could see that it was the wrong thickness, that it was just watery red.

I laughed to myself, *Do not be too full of confidence, Anya!* But in my head I had called myself by my old name, and this made me feel shaken, even more – I could not pretend to be a new person, in this new life. And it was the same, I kept on feeling some presence behind me, calling to me, and I thought to turn slowly, to show that I was not afraid, but when I got all of the way around, I could see that I had made a mess in the kitchen, and the pile of dishes and pans was a huge black shadow beside the sink, and of course! You are not a wife, Anya! It had begun to rain again and I did not dare to look outside, to the trees where the plastic bags that caught in the branches waved like flags: the English countryside that was grey, nothing alike to the pictures, nothing alike to what John had promised.

The second squid burst, more exciting this time, because I had seen that John would be home in two hours, and maybe he might even come home early. I knew that I must have something for my John, my babylove, that my skills *cooking, cleaning, sensuality,* would please him, would make him more happy and kinder, so I tried to make the mangled white bodies presentable, on the nicest plate that I could find in the cupboard, it was only chipped in one place. I put the squid in a kind of pile, four on the bottom and then three, one balanced carefully by itself, trying to hide the rips in the white flesh, while the juices from the meat and vegetables dripped down in tears. I wiped the blood from around the meat, so that the plate stayed white, and then I stood back to observe my dish.

I sat on a chair and looked at the food for quite a long time, now and then dabbing at the white plate as more red juice leaked down into a puddle, making sure to save the bright whiteness.

John came home at 10.45 p.m., and that was when the dish had gone very cold, even though I kept heating it so it was steaming again. Now the bodies had begun to turn yellow from the reheating, and they looked sticky, like glue or a wound that is bad. After a few hours, I had given up on cleaning the red, so the septic bodies were swimming in juice like crimson.

'Babylove!' I shouted, and I ran to turn on the kitchen light, in case John would be angry with me for sitting in the darkness again. 'I have made you a delicious meal.'

I smelt his smoke, but he did not follow my voice and John, my babylove, he must have been so tired, because he shouted to me, 'I got kebab,' and nothing more.

And then I could hear him going away, into the shower, and I heard him turning the water on, mumbling to himself, and staggering a little while he was taking off his clothes and, where the room was bright now, I saw that the rain was falling on the window, very heavy and fast. My hands were bunched, and I unclenched them, doing some calming breathing, but I could hear thunder rumbling from far away, and I saw that there were veins standing pronounced in my hands already, and that my fingers were red and hard, dry, old-woman hands: *where was Mama? John was taking all my gifts from me.* I was looking at the rain that was slapping the window so angrily that it seemed it might be a person, wanting to come right through, and I remembered my tato, the prisoner in his little sickness bed, and then, when the lightning flashed, I saw John's heavy shape, moving around in the front room. John put on the television very loudly, and the shadows began to jump around in the silver light, surrounding John like sea monsters.

I slammed the red mixture, and the little white bodies all together and into a ball, the legs spurting out at some strange angles, red still inside. I looked at this shape, red and white, fatty and like it would be living, surrounded by old rubbish in the pedal bin, and I realised, *Look there, Mama; this mess looks so very much alike to my John's human heart.*

Everything was changed in my mind, so I made a test the next night.

John would always be saying that he didn't like to take his pills, so I said, 'John, John, you must take your pills, my babylove,' and I kept on saying, like a good wife, even though he was watching his favourite film, the *Die Hard* film. He still has a VHS player that he uses for this film only and he repeats the lines to himself, 'Welcome to the party, Pal,' very serious.

'John, John, John,' I said, 'you must take your pills.' Until finally, he shouted, 'Don't tell me what to do, you bloody bitch,' and he threw the pill bottle at me and it popped open, just like that, and then the pills leaked all over the floor.

'John!' I said, and I looked down at the little white pills, and thought, *Oh no! The pills are dirty now; think of it this way: those pills will probably do my babylove more harm than good.* So I threw all of the pills into the bin.

When I saw my babylove John stamping around the kitchen in his slippers a few days later and pouring out drawers so that all the items were a mess across the kitchen table – all the work items, thick gloves, twine that was twisted like an angry face, many, many papers and notes that John had written to himself, then a blue ball that bounced away and into a dark corner – and I said, 'What are you looking for, babylove?'

And he said, 'Where are my fucking pills?'

And I said, 'I thought that you didn't want them, John. I threw them into the bin,' and it was then that John stared at me for the longest second and I saw that his face was really bright red already, and then, while I was watching, it turned even brighter red, it was like a blistering boil, and John grabbed me, and shook my shoulders – he squeezed my flesh tightly.

'You bitch,' he whispered, into my face, and some of his breath went into my mouth. And I thought of what Mama had said before I left to marry John, maybe John *was* the same as my tato, just a son-of-a-dog bastard, but then I shook the thoughts away, I had to, and I remembered; this was my John, my babylove!

And later, when he wouldn't let me have any of the fish and chips and iced yellow doughnuts that he had, that was all right to me, because I wasn't that hungry anyway, and I thought about what the doctor with the soft gloves had said about me taking care, and how the rain had fallen so fast on the surgery window, the tree with the black arms, and I just gave my love John that extra portion, and I poured salt and vinegar on the chips so that they were all soggy wet and sparkling, like romantic stars in the sky, just how he likes them. And instead of watching the *Die Hard* man saving everybody's lives, I sat and I watched my babylove eat all of that food, looking at the little dribble on his chin and the sticky around his mouth.

I couldn't sleep, and every night I watched John snoring and grunting, and wondered, Will his heart stop tonight or tomorrow morning? Will it stop while he fixes some plumbing, or at The Brass Cross? Will John die in my very own arms? I spent a lot of time looking at the items in the death trunk, and reading the leaflets over and over. *Cooking, cleaning and sensuality* – I thought of what Mama had said: could I have really stayed at home, worked in the local restaurant? Mama, with her tired hands, her sad voice. I added other items to the trunk: some powerful bleach, and a letter that had been delivered from the kind doctor that asked for John to come into the hospital for a check-up, and a repeat prescription of his pills. The paperwork inside the trunk was now quite a lot and I looked through the sheets, checking all of the terms and conditions.

I was scared that if John collapsed outside somewhere, he would be rushed to hospital and surrounded by all of those fussy people and the nancy boys that he hated. I could sense how angry that would make my babylove; he hated to be told what to do, to be forced into spots that he was not happy in.

John just wanted to live his own life; he wanted to be free, that is what he told me.

In the end, it happened on an ordinary Sunday, just ten days after I had made John the squid meal – the day when everything was changed. John had not gone to the pub that day because it was very grey outside, and swamp light went across the front room. The storm was over but the air was wet when I opened the window. The tea towel that had been drying on the sill was still sopping. I saw John lying back on his reclining chair, like a toad, my babylove.

The oven had been needing a very good scrub since I had arrived at Paradise Block and, even though John was not interested in eating the very nice meals that I had thought to make him, I wanted to keep everything clean.

John was watching the television and eating a television lunch meal, which I had taken from packets and assembled for him. It was pie and chips with blood puddings, a food that does not look red like blood at all, but is black, dark like an eye.

The oven was very dirty and I wondered at myself for letting it get so filthy and disgusting; what had I been thinking about? I began by loosening the dirt that clung to the bottom of the oven, right inside. There was a smear of red sauce on the front of the glass, so sticky and perfectly formed that it looked like it could be lifted right off. I became obsessed by this cleaning although, I will have to say, I did hear something coming from the front room, a little like John was calling me from where he was sat, eating his food. I was fingering this red sauce, the orange part where it was thin, and the deep red where the sauce was thick, and I considered to myself that the sound was almost definitely coming from the television. I started to hum in a gentle way, and I thought to play my Whitney Houston CD. I needed to get the job done, and cleaning is one of my special interests, so I became very busy and engrossed.

When I pulled the tray out of the oven I exclaimed because there were little pools of fat around the rim, gathering, thick and yellow. I must have been cooking many greasy foods for John babylove, because the tray was filthy with fat! Again, I was hearing this strange sound, strangled and angry, but I was so engrossed, removing the fat and thinking about how Mama would look at me if she could see me now, scratching with a scourer, and then with my fingernails, a little frantic, when the fat would not move; I wanted to wash it all, to hide the yellow of the grime. Would Mama tell me that I had failed? My fingers were slippery now, and the water ran away from them, like I was wearing a protective plastic glove. I was transfixed, hearing those yelps only slightly, and watching droplets of water sticking on to my hands, my wedding ring was a crystal amongst many other sparkling diamonds, all looking like other, different lives.

In our flat, the telephone was in the kitchen, so I soon saw John, my babylove, dragging himself along the floor, where he would be flipping over on to his back, like a big fish, caught in the black wave, and saying, 'Annie, help me, please.'

Of course, I turned the tap off right away. John was green already, a murky sea-deep kind of green, with purple edges. John's eyes were bulging.

'Oh, John!' I said. 'Your heart!'

And John grabbed my hand, but the fat had made my skin so slippery that it slithered right out of his grip, and I ran until I was backed right against the wall. That was only a few steps because our kitchen was very small.

John stretched his arm towards me. 'Help me!' he said. 'Help me, Anya!'

For a moment our eyes were together, but then his outstretched arm, which was waving away, distracted me. Oh, such sadness I felt, that same arm that had, for so many times, held me still, in a gentle caress, as John performed the sex acts upon me.

Cooking, cleaning, sensuality.
Red, green, blue.
Anya Kolesnik, very thick.

Tears were springing into my eyes, running down my face, until I had become quite wet in my grief, but this seemed to make John angry, my babylove, and he went into a mad frenzy; all kinds of swear words came out of his mouth, and some creamy spit, as though the fats were all coming out of him, and I felt very afraid then, because I was not sure whether he could stand up, even though he was flat on his back holding on to his chest.

'You bitch,' John said, and these were the last things I ever heard from his mouth, because after that he quickly died.

I finished cleaning the oven with more tears exploding from my eyes, and when I was nearly done, I saw a small, decaying tentacle with dirty yellow rot squeezing out of its suckers. The tentacle had turned grey-blue, and it was disgusting, but I kept looking at it, remembering Mama, while I scooted around John's body and to the pedal bin, where I dropped the disgusting item and shut it away with the rest of John's heart, right at the bottom of the bin, all covered in beer cans and sweet packets, and plastic containers from takeaway dinners.

I am Annie, a good wife and woman with skills in cooking and cleaning and sensuality. This is my story of the broken heart, cut into pieces.

I did not want to keep the flat in Paradise Block, and when John died that day, the weight of his thrashing body on the floor made some more cracks appear on the walls, all over the ceiling; the flat looked as though it would burst open and fall into dust all around me. There were the cracks, the heart in the bin, and the oven, still dirty, so after the ambulance had gone, I took the bank cards, where John keeps all his money and savings, the precious earnings from his caring for Paradise Block, and I left with my things in a black bag. It would be so tragically lucky that the nice insurance woman had given me such comfort on that lonely day, just when I was starting to suspect the worst, because then, when that money comes to me, I will be able to buy my own flat in Plum Regis, just how John would have wanted it. Mama will be so pleased, and she will see that I was right, that I had to find my own way through the world.

Even a long time after his death, I still speak to John, my babylove, and I remember all the things that he would say to me, before we met – the times that we might have had together, in the English countryside, or at the seaside, shopping at the gardening centre – which is what could have happened, if he had not had to go to The Brass Cross every day. I remember John, as I wanted him to be, the English gentleman that I had imagined, that long time ago, and then, in my head, we are so happy together – John is my sweet babylove.

In the night-time, I wear my sensual gown. I put my feet into John's slippers and up on to the dashboard of the silver car that I bought in John's memory. John was always complaining about how he could not afford a car and how this was stopping him from doing the things that he wanted to do. He told me that we would go on all kinds of trips if he could have afforded a car. And now, it is as though John is travelling with me. I will be stopping high up on a green hill, when the sun is setting, watching out for my babylove's spirit, anyplace amongst the trees. From this little park on the hillside, I can see a lot of planes flying over and I watch their bellies and arms, imagining that I will fly away one day, not back to Mama and my yellow-white room, but to some other place.

On the day that John was to be buried, I saw my babylove in this park. He was as a young man, smoothed away, not green or blue or red, freckles were across his cheeks like a handful of sand. This young-man-John was leant up against a rusted sunflower-coloured playing frame, but looking very smart and professional, wearing the uniform of an air pilot. We were watching the planes together; this must have been a special interest for this young-man-John. I waved to him and he raised one hand, held it still and smiled softly.

The rain is sometimes falling, but the raindrops are away from me, sliding down the body of my car, or on the windscreen, and the light comes in spikes. I look at my shimmering hands as I touch the runaway drops on the windscreen.

Still, I do not get wet.

Note

The caretaker is cleaning out the old man's flat, listening to music on her phone. Even though the caretaker hasn't seen much of the old man, there's been more of him over the past few years, and the caretaker realises that she will miss him. There had been very loud laughter, vibrating out into the corridor; she'd seen him appear flickeringly on his balcony, all grey and white, a mucky snowfall of a man. The caretaker looks over the car park – there is a tree; someone has tied old CDs to pieces of wool and hung them from the bare branches where they flash and wink in the dreamy light. The CDs are dancing in the breeze like peaks of water. The caretaker reminds herself to take her scissors down later; she'll stand amongst the purple, red and green, ready to snip the magic from the tree. She pulls her hair into a determined knot on top of her head, but still feels a little sting of sadness. Somehow, it had seemed like the old man was getting younger: heading towards youth, rather than shuffling towards the more shadowy place.

But anyway, there isn't much to take from the flat, and the house clearance men handle it all quite roughly, as though they are scared that they will cry if they linger for too long; their brows are furrowed and they glance their hands over their stubbled chins many times until the skin is red and sore. They take the pair of slumped old armchairs and the long-necked lamp. The caretaker juts her jaw, wonders how the house clearance men can deal with it, if they get upset each time, what mementos of life might set them off – the balled heel of a slipper; the cooking instructions for pepperoni pizza, cut from the back of a packet; an expensive set of dust-capped wedding china. Between songs, the caretaker can hear her mother walking around, out in the corridor; her mother uses a stick now.

The caretaker is about to leave the flat, to find the correct key on the big set that jangles like octopus legs by her side and lock the door. The flat would settle into complete silence, maybe for years. But before the caretaker leaves, she sees the book, down in the toothy lip of the radiator. This is a fat notebook, its spine cracked all over with white worms, and its yellow pages fanned out like the hair of a messy little boy. The caretaker runs her hand over the pages; the front of the book is labelled 'Grisco–Cornflower Charter', and inside, every single page is covered with tiny, intricate notes, in several different handwritings and inks. Before she locks up the flat, humming and sighing a little bit, remembering the old man and his booming voice, the caretaker flips to the last page where the words form a kind of whirlpool; they circle each other and shrink and grow

        Tomorrow   *paradise*
   Tomorrow!
            We'll go down to the fair
Candyfloss   *rain*   new shoes!
     Yes
                no stopping us
       tomorrow.

The caretaker packs away her cleaning equipment, on to the wheeled caddy; the bubbly mop water slops with rainbow colours. She looks twice over her shoulder at the dark flat, turns the long silver key in the lock, and listens to the crack of the latch. She puts the notebook in her satchel with her phone and the headphones; the custard-coloured rubber gloves; her mother's medication, pale and chalky; a chocolate egg, fondant inside – there's a lot to do and so, the caretaker continues her day.

Acknowledgements

My deepest thanks to my agent, Zoe Ross, who understood and deftly championed *Paradise Block* from the start. To my magnificent editor, Leonora Craig Cohen, who had a special way of sorting through the tangled nest of my mind, and who endlessly improved this book with her intelligent and kind perspective. Thank you to my simply lovely publicist, Anna-Marie Fitzgerald, as well as Hannah Westland and Graeme Hall at Serpent's Tail. It has been overwhelmingly wonderful to work with you all.

Thank you to my beloved parents, Russell, Pepe & Julia: Pepe who enthusiastically dragged me out of bed to write hungover essays; Russell who should take credit for a large share of my best quirks; and Julia who inspired me with stories from the depths of the family vault, (and who didn't buy a new TV when ours got nicked). Thank you to my Granny and Grandpa, Elizabeth and David – for supporting me and for being special people in my life. Thank you, Nanny, Barbara, who always has the best stories, and who prodded me up the treacherous hill. Thank you, Jim – my brilliant brother, who always said the right thing, and who once reacted to my rejection misery by making ten strangers give me a 'giant spoon' in the smoking area outside Green Door Store. Thank you to my great love, Jamie, who listened to my fears, stubbornly forced me to believe in myself, and who wore holey shoes with me for nearly a decade.

Thank you to the supporters of this book – most particularly, Livia Franchini, who has consistently gone out of her way to help me and who has loving kindness in every tendril of her bouncy hair – thank you. Rosie Adams, who officially made me want to be a Cool Writer at the Goth Pub off Tottenham Court Rd, and who I will always love. The Writer's Circus – Madeline Denny, Harrison Perry, Karen and Peter Vincent-Jones & Sally Osbourne – you all kept me going and inspired me. Thank you Dizz Tate, Thom James and Charlotte Heather. The Write Process Group – Julie Bull, Dominique Delight, Chris Williams, Nina Cullinane, Hong Dam and Phil Morgan. Kiri Crequer, Ishita Mandrekar, Isaac Liddle, Katie Guastapaglia, Laura Grace, Joe Curtis & Rosey Wilkin. The Nancy Writing Group. Rachael and Luther Adams. Jeff Scott. Mike Pearson. Emma Gaskin. Thank you to my teachers at the University of Westminster: Monica Germana, John O'Donoghue, Matt Morrison, and to Susanna Jones at Royal Holloway. Thank you to TLC Free Reads, Creative Future, The Arvon Foundation, New Writing South, The PHC, The Spice Girls, The NHS, the great pubs of Brighton and Hove, Jubilee Library, & City College Access to Higher Education English Literature, where I wore a pillowcase as a skirt, ate sugar sachets in the cafeteria for lunch, and found my first ever seed of confidence after writing an okay essay on *Hamlet*. And thank you to my ever-enduring best pals, who know exactly who they are.

Bibliographical Note

Many of the stories collected here appeared in an earlier form in the following publications:

'Eggs'– Longlisted for the Galley Beggar Short Story Prize 2019

'The Flea-Trap' – *Extra Teeth Magazine*

'You'– *Boon Magazine, With Regard to Modernity, Paper and Ink, Milk and Honey, Leopardskin and Limes, Girl Love Zine*

'Hungry'– *Spam Zine*

'Doctor Sharpe'– *Galavant Literary Magazine, With Regard to Modernity, SFWP Quarterly*

'Black, Dark Hill' – *Popshot Quarterly*, published as 'Boats'

'John's Bride'– *The Squawkback*